THE TALES OF AMCRONOS
BOOK 1

THE KNIGHTS OF
TORIN

COLSON ROSA

THE KNIGHTS OF TORIN

ILLUSTRATIONS BY RACHEL AND ETHAN LAMB

COVER ART AND MAP BY JODY BALL

Mom and Dad,

Thank you for helping and inspiring me. You encouraged me to continue even when I struggled to get my ideas organized and on paper. Your patience throughout the editing of this book was a real blessing. You truly are a gift from God!

Table of Contents

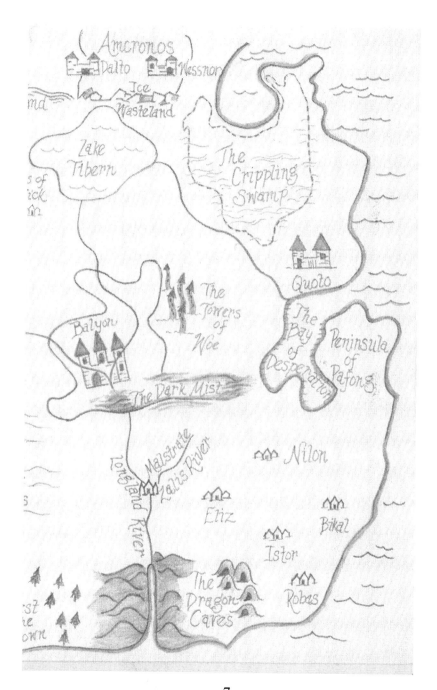

PROLOGUE

Light and darkness never truly coexist. There is often a struggle between them. Some say good always prevails, but even if that were true, it always comes with a price.

In a small town on the outskirts of a forest, the blacksmith's anvil burned hot. The hammer stroked the metal skillfully with a clash. The sound of rushing water sizzled through the shop as it extinguished the raging fire. The blacksmith's brow was laden with sweat and his bones ached.

The man lived in a humble home with his wife and son. Although their space was limited, they found room for those in need. Since lanterns were their main source of light, the house smelled of oil. It was obvious that the house was old, because the daub which held it together had crumbled, leaving gaps in the framework. Since the roof was covered in straw, occasionally drops of rain and whips of wind could be felt within.

One day, a knight ventured into the town, tired from a long journey, his feet painfully sore. In an alley outside the bakery, the blacksmith's son, Lavrin, noticed the knight and offered him some bread. He then invited him to his home, knowing his father would greet the traveler as a friend.

When Lavrin arrived home, his mother noticed he returned without bread, which made her quite upset. Lavrin explained that he had given it to the knight and had invited him here. His mother gladly welcomed him in, and soon the knight was set up in the loft. It was the only place they had for him to sleep.

It was supper time, so the blacksmith's wife prepared some steaming rabbit stew spiced up with what little parsley they had. Lavrin's father offered the knight one of the three chairs around their small table, while he insisted upon sitting on a stump he had brought in from their woodpile. The knight greatly enjoyed the simple stew, for it had been many weeks since he had eaten a well-prepared meal.

The knight thanked the family for their hospitality and told them of the order he followed. He shared of the

King of Light and of his compassion for the world. The boy was especially awed by the stories about the King's knights, who spread their faith and won battles for their cause.

The knight stayed with the blacksmith's family for several weeks. On many occasions, he accompanied Lavrin and his pet terrier, Vin, throughout the countryside. Soon enough, he began to teach Lavrin how to use a sword and wield it like a warrior. Eventually, the knight needed to return to the King's service. He left Lavrin with a knife as a token of their friendship and blessed the family. The knife was simple yet was decorated with a special symbol - the emblem of the King. The design of the emblem was a sword with the rays of the sun shining behind it. It would be a gift young Lavrin would cherish always.

A week later, a sudden and unexpected commotion arose in the town. Enemies of the King came armed with clubs, swords, and axes - a task force bent on hate. They went from house to house, threatening anyone who refused to proclaim the evil Natas as lord. Master of lies, hater of love, Natas was notorious in the land for forcing the people into cruel submission. Those who resisted Natas' demands were robbed, their houses and everything in them burned. Some were so afraid and willing to submit that they gave what little they had to Natas' men, hoping they would leave.

When the loud knock came at the door of the blacksmith's house, there was no answer, no reply. The savages broke in, only to see the family eating. The blacksmith seized his axe and the house erupted into chaos.

CHAPTER 1

TRUE BROTHERS

Lavrin walked over and sat on a lonely tree trunk. He could not stop thinking of that day five years ago, the day when everything had gone so horribly wrong.

******

Swoosh. A black arrow flew right by him as he ate his first bite of supper. Swoosh, swoosh. Two arrows zoomed so close to his father that it was amazing that they missed. His father shoved Lavrin down the hall. "Run, Lavrin. Get to the forest!" his father yelled.

Understanding the urgency of the situation, young Lavrin desperately ran to his room and started frantically packing his few possessions into a burlap sack. He crammed in a full canteen and a small knife, and then pulled his dark brown hood over his brunette hair.

While he slipped on his boots, he remembered Vin, his small gray terrier. He opened the door, finding much to his relief Vin outside, begging for his owner. Lavrin felt him tremble as he picked him up and tucked him under his arm. He grabbed his bag and walking stick, and fled out the open window. Luckily, the invaders barged into Lavrin's room right as he escaped into the shadows. Before moving any further, he gazed in shock as his humble home burst into flames, black smoke spiraling into the evening sky.

With tears in his eyes, he wondered if he would ever see his family again. How would he survive without them? A tear began its descent down his cheek as he contemplated his new reality. He hoped he would never forget the faces of the two people he loved most in the world.

******

"What's going on in there?" questioned Lavrin's companion, tapping him on the skull.

"Oh, sorry," answered Lavrin, startled back into reality.

"Thinking about it again?" his friend asked.

"How did you…"

"I've been with you forever. I know."

Lavrin looked at him sheepishly. Calix Windrider had become a loyal friend who had a story much like Lavrin's own. Losing both parents to the cruel Black Plague at the age of twelve, Calix had also become a wanderer, and had eventually stumbled upon Lavrin along the outskirts of the forest.

It seemed like an eternity ago, the time they first met. It had been a long day; Lavrin had used the little money he had to buy a loaf of bread in a town just outside the forest veil. Six months had passed since the disaster that had changed his life. Calix had set up his tent some sixty paces inside the forest. Seeking a shortcut back to his own tent, Lavrin had somehow gone astray in the mist and found Calix's tent instead. Calix had introduced himself and welcomed Lavrin to sit by the fire. Thankful for the hospitality, Lavrin offered Calix some of his bread.

As they sat, Lavrin enlightened his new friend about the King and his kingdom across the sea, at least the way he remembered the knight telling it. With something now to aspire toward, the two decided that together they would join the King's army, relishing the idea of a life filled with adventure and purpose. Though the chance had not arisen yet, they clung to hope that it would one day.

Looking at them side by side, no one would ever mistake them for brothers, though they acted as if they were. Calix's dark skin was quite a contrast from fair Lavrin. Since they had first met, they had stayed side by side, helping each other and training together, just as true brothers would. A bond of spirit and soul united them at

13

their very core. Now at the age of sixteen, it was as if they had never been apart.

Through thick and thin, they had been at each other's side. Many times they had been stranded in the forest together, low on food and swamped by the rain. Nevertheless, they survived the elements and grew stronger through adversity.

Avoided by many, the Forest of Bane was not easy to live in. Thick thorns and twisting branches seemed to cross every path. Throughout the day and well into the night, chirps and squeals could be heard. The forest animals barely allowed even a single moment of silence. Truly, there were many different obstacles to making one's home here. This forest was not suitable for ordinary people, but Lavrin and Calix made it possible – two boys without a family or much of a future.

Overcoming the enormous odds against them, the boys were tremendously pleased with themselves. They had constructed a house in a tall, thick oak tree. The tree house was minimal in size, but it suited them fine. On their own, they survived a hard yet adventurous existence. Often, they would go to town and trade their forest trappings and wild berries with the local vendors in exchange for a little of this and that. Nonetheless, they never let their dream of serving the King fade.

The King of Light once ruled Amcronos from his home in the Haven Realm. One of his nobles, Natas, had been unhappy with the power the King had granted him. He gathered an army to form a rebellion, for he considered himself wiser than the King. After a great war in the Haven Realm, the forces of the King prevailed against Natas. The King had no choice but to banish him and his men from the Haven Realm. Natas wanted revenge, so he set out to deceive the citizens of Amcronos, where he had been banished.

Eventually seizing control of Amcronos, Natas ruled the land with an iron fist. Although he was very intelligent, he was corrupt in heart and soul. The only way he kept the people happy with his rule was by filling their minds with lies.

He spread roots of deceit as he cunningly dispatched his henchmen throughout Amcronos, trying to corrupt both men and creatures. He never could defeat the King, for the King's power stretched far above his own. Yet he did succeed in turning many away from the King and into aiding his sinister plot.

The Forests of Bane and Torin were now back under the control of the King of Light. Through the work of his messengers, he had reclaimed the northwestern portion of Amcronos, from Hessington to Vanswick. The King of Light loved the lands he ruled and always did what was right. His lands flourished agriculturally, while Natas's land prospered from mining and laborious work.

Lavrin and Calix were glad that they lived outside of Natas' lands. They only had to worry about getting supplies from the market to last another few months.

There were two options for Lavrin and Calix when it came to going to the market. Though they did not need supplies often, it was troublesome when they did, because both places were more than a day's travel away. Because they had little money, they fished, hunted and gathered what they could from the forest, and put off a trip as long as possible.

Ken Van was the farther of the two towns, and its people were cruel and drove hard bargains. Furthermore, they profited from slavery. Lavrin and Calix had heard that many were pushing for the town to join Natas. This was not a place they wanted to visit. The fair, decent city known as Saberlin was closer than Ken Van, so it was the more likely choice.

The friends were sitting at their hand-carved table while Vin was sniffing out a squirrel somewhere not too far away. "Our supplies are dwindling, Calix. I think we should go to the market," said Lavrin.

He looked around the room as he spoke. The makeshift cabinets hung loosely on the wall by several nails, and the table had a broken leg. Lavrin wished they could do more to repair their home, but the harsh weather kept it always in a state of disrepair.

"You're right, our spices are getting low. Besides, I could use a new shirt." Calix looked down at his tattered shirt, then back to Lavrin.

"Let's head to Saberlin, then," Lavrin said. "We can work there three days or so and buy our supplies the next.

16

Vin can guard; he has done it before. We'll need to leave early in the morning."

"Hopefully you won't sleep in this time."

The next day came upon them quickly. Lavrin made sure Vin was placed on watch. He only hoped the dog would not wander off and get lost as he had done many times before. Calix placed blankets, food and their limited weapons in leather bags and threw one to Lavrin, who slung it over his shoulder.

Earlier in the year, Calix and Lavrin had made the trek to Saberlin. It was a large city filled with men of various trades. The loyal lord of the city kept a small garrison of troops to ensure peace with the nearby lands. The lord lived humbly and well below his means. He used as much of his money as he could toward the betterment of his people, and it showed.

Each citizen had food, clothes, money, a job, a home and a set of rights. It was a glorious time for Saberlin because the people were happy, and the city's industry, art and knowledge flourished through trade and commerce. It was a city well worth the journey.

Climbing down the old rope ladder, Lavrin and Calix looked up and smiled to Vin, who was sitting calmly above them. "Goodbye, boy," Lavrin called as his feet hit the ground.

Vin responded with a loud bark. The two started on their way with the morning sun shining upon them. Vin, though easily distracted, was a very capable protector of the tree house. He would fend off all wild creatures of the forest with true devotion. He already longed for his masters' return.

"I would say, for two orphaned boys living on scraps, we have made quite the life for ourselves," Calix said.

"Yes, we have," Lavrin remarked. "Still, I am sure we could be doing more. I feel like we are pebbles among a bed of rocks. No one even knows we are here or cares, for that matter. Do you think the world has abandoned us, Calix?"

Calix shrugged. "If anything, it's the other way around. We may have abandoned society, but that's no reason to be downcast. Cheer up. We'll buy some extra wood and nails to repair our home. If we spend our money wisely, we can get enough goods to last us several more months. The road to progress is slow. We're still alive and that's what matters."

Lavrin nodded. "Quite so, my friend. I would not have it any other way. There is something about living in the forest that is refreshing and pure. The world is bogged down by taxes, scoundrels and the worries of life. We are free to live how we choose. Freedom may not be luxurious, but you and Vin are all I need to be happy."

"I feel like you know me better than I know myself. Do you have the furs?'

"I knew you would forget them under your bed, so I grabbed them with mine."

Calix grinned and lifted some of the pelts from his friend's shoulders. "It is a long trek. We don't need you carrying all of the weight now, do we?" Lavrin nudged him. The two smelled the crisp pine as they maneuvered around the underbrush, talking as they went.

CHAPTER 2

SABERLIN

As Lavrin and Calix continued their journey toward Saberlin, they grew increasingly excited with each step. What new items would they find in Saberlin this time? All in all, the journey to Saberlin was never a boring trek, as their minds were filled with the hope of something new.

Stopping once to camp by a creek and rising early the next morning, they anticipated their arrival at Saberlin to be about midday. They made good time by eating on the way. This part of the forest was filled with wild berries, and although they were not incredibly sweet, they were nevertheless satisfying. This kept their stomachs content while they walked on.

They reached the town about midday, as anticipated. They could not help but notice that much had changed.

Stone walls were built up high, guards were posted and a moat was being added. It looked more like a fortified castle than the pleasant city they remembered. Going inside, they noticed the ruler's residence had changed from a small mansion to a castle-like structure with three huge towers. It seemed that the people were being neglected and poorly treated. Lavrin and Calix expected something was out of the ordinary.

An old woman walked by them. Calix asked, "Pardon me, ma'am?"

"Yes," she said in a croaky voice.

"What is going on here in Saberlin? Even the town emblem has changed."

"Who are you?" the woman asked, cautious of the outsiders.

"I am Calix from the house of Windrider. We have come to get supplies, and noticed the recent amount of construction."

"Oh yes, Windrider... your father was a merchant, wasn't he? I have not heard news of your father in years. Well, here's the sad truth: the good ruler of Saberlin, Bevlin, has died. Zekern, his oldest son, has taken his place. It has been rumored that he even killed his younger brother to ensure he would be the lord of this city. He has encouraged slavery, gambling, violence, and everything his father hated, anything that would gain him more power and control over the people."

21

"How awful; he obviously does not waste time," Lavrin said.

"That's not all," she continued, glancing around to make sure no guards were in the area. "He uses his money and power to purchase wives and slaves. No one has the means to face him. Many have either fled the city or have at least considered it. I don't want to leave as I have lived here all my life, and my husband, the mason, is feverishly working on Zekern's many projects. Besides, I am getting too old now. Though I am not as limber as I used to be, my keen eyes have not failed me. Zekern has many spies and guards throughout the city. They hear all and report everything to him, even what is bought and sold. If you owe anything to him, he will force you to pay or make you his slave. This is another reason why we cannot leave, as we owe him money as well."

******

As Lavrin and Calix told her their story, Vin patrolled the perimeter of the tree house. He was desperately trying to find something to do. The only sounds around were the birds chirping, mocking him for being so bored. There was not much he could do about it because he could not fly, an ability he always wished to have. He imagined himself the terror terrier of the skies, swooping down upon the unsuspecting vermin of the forest and causing such a fright that they would all flee in his midst. Yet it was just a dream. Vin dared not leave his post.

He had seen it all before, the same shadows falling on the thickets. There was the wandering fawn, straying just to the edge of her mother's watchful eyes. The woodpeckers were more quiet than usual. Vin could only hope this rarity would last.

Like a guardian angel, Vin watched the comings and goings of the forest from his platform. Vin could have easily appreciated the joyous dance of the roses in the wind or the sapling stretching to grab hold of the sunlight, but he was too bored to notice. He hoped Lavrin and Calix would not be long, lest he do something foolish.

******

"You would do well to watch yourself while you are here," the old woman said. "I doubt you will have any trouble finding a few days' worth of work for yourselves. My husband probably could use the help. Make sure you leave before the week is over, because Zekern's band of thugs will likely have arrived by then. They are always looking for some excuse to raise up a ruckus with young men such as yourselves."

"Thank you for the advice," Calix said.

"It's nothing. This town really needs help, as you can see." She sighed. "I have to get on with my chores. I wish you the best." She turned and walked away just as a group of guards rounded the corner.

"Do you think things are as bad as she says? It seems hard to believe how much has happened in the last five months," Calix pondered aloud.

"I believe they are. She seemed sincere," Lavrin said. "Besides, look at all the evidence. The guards at the front gate sure glared at us when we came into town. Come, we need to talk with her husband."

The boys remembered that the town mason was kind and truthful, a quality tradesman. He was a part of a mason guild which was supportive of the King. The mason was someone they could trust. They hoped to help him and find out what they could do in service of the King.

Heading down the street toward the mason's shop, they continued to notice changes to the city. They wondered whether the mason would lose his job if Zekern learned of his loyalty to the King.

While on their way, Lavrin and Calix heard a commotion gathering near the market. Two men, one quite large, were flipping carts, wrestling the guards and causing a huge uproar. The bold men mocked the guards, and the larger threw a guard into the mud. The other guards reacted by drawing their swords and making threats. The townsfolk poked their heads out from behind windows and doors to see what all the noise was about. Though the guards outnumbered the duo, they struggled to fight against them. The incredibly audacious troublemakers unarmed their foes and sent them slamming into the ground. The guards, unharmed except for their pride, called for reinforcements.

Lavrin and Calix gazed past the crowd to see a hooded figure enter an alleyway. They could tell he was up to something and decided to follow. They pursued the figure to an abandoned house on a nearby corner. They then saw two guards patrolling the street, heading toward the house. Lavrin suddenly met them in their path.

"What are you doing here?" Lavrin yelled. "Haven't you heard there's a commotion in the market? You had better go help before it gets violent." The guards rushed to the adjacent street and lifted their shields.

"Why did you do that?" Calix asked.

"We need to find out what's going on here. I have a feeling something suspicious is taking place." Lavrin paused. "Something that trouble in the market would be a good cover for. Come on."

The two silently crept around the house and listened through the back door. Inside, they heard whispers but could not understand what was being said. They peered through a crack in the wooden planks to see a woman holding manuscripts which she handed to the mysterious figure. He then rushed out the door and headed toward some trees near the city wall, unaware of his two followers. When he reached the wall, he climbed up a tree. Once on top of the wall, he cast a rope down the other side. He then hurried into the forest for cover.

Close behind, Lavrin and Calix climbed down the rope with haste and entered the forest. Like tigers stalking in the grass, Lavrin and Calix suddenly backed up against a tree as the man stopped and looked around. They figured this was some meeting point, since the man was carefully looking through the trees for something or someone.

Little did they know, the two men who had stirred up the commotion in the market were now right behind them, and one signaled to the other to surround them. As Lavrin peeked from behind the tree, a man wrestled him to the ground. Lavrin punched and kicked, but he was overtaken and bound. Calix tried to assist, but felt a blow across the back and collapsed.

As Lavrin's and Calix's heads were covered and their hands tied, the two captors called to their partner. The three traveled further into the forest, leading the captives to their camp. Lavrin and Calix had been too consumed in their task to realize they also had been followed out of Saberlin.

Now they were being taken, Lavrin assumed to the trio's base. Along the way, he felt the cold wind pass by his face as his feet stumbled over roots and puddles. It was hard to keep quiet as thoughts, hopes and fears raced through his head. Each step was like a mile, and Lavrin's sore body ached. He assumed they were in the Forest of Torin.

The Forest of Torin lay southeast of Saberlin. The only thing that separated it from their home in the Forest of Bane was a small valley. It was called the Mud Ridge Valley, because of the rain which often poured into it.

After they arrived at their captors' camp, Lavrin and Calix were momentarily left in a tent. They tried to calm themselves with deep breaths, but the thought of being captured and tried by these mysterious rogues was too much for them. They overheard voices talking quietly outside.

"What should we do with them? They may be spies. They could escape and warn Zekern of our whereabouts." At that, Lavrin stopped breathing.

"Why do we need to be so cautious?" a sharp voice questioned. "We know nothing about them."

Then a third voice commanded, "We shall question them, then make the final decision."

******

Two posts, short enough for the prisoners to touch the ground, were carried to the place of the interrogation. As they were brought out, Calix and Lavrin stared into the leader's eyes. They were full of passion and sincerity, gleaming blue like the sky. They could tell he was well-shaven for a ruffian, which they presumed him to be. There was an air of mystery and curiosity about this man.

Lavrin and Calix did not know what to do, think or say. As they walked toward their posts, all was quiet. Ropes were bound around their arms and legs; they knew there would be no escape. The grilling was about to begin.

As he felt the pressure rise, Lavrin felt courage rise in him as well. He would tell them the truth and nothing else. No lies or scandal. He looked over at Calix reassuringly.

To break the silence, the leader of the small group spoke. "I am Chan. I lead these men. Tell us who you are."

Calix gulped. Could this man be trusted? After carefully thinking of the right thing to say, Calix was ready to respond. "My name is Calix and this is my friend, Lavrin. We are simple rangers of the forest. We do not want to harm you."

"What would two rangers be doing in Saberlin?" Chan asked.

"We have traveled from the Forest of Bane to resupply in Saberlin. Nothing more than that," Lavrin said.

Chan gave him a glare, unconvinced. "Who do you serve? Clearly you have had contact with the rest of the world."

"We serve the King and live for him. We were surprised to find that Saberlin no longer serves the King, and a new leader rules there."

"We were already aware of this."

"We serve the King, and he will harm you if you choose to harm us."

"Which King do you speak of?" Chan asked sharply, unwilling to respond to Lavrin's comment.

To make sure they understood, Lavrin dared to speak the King's motto, which had been outlawed by Natas. "The great King of Light, may he live and reign forever, and may his followers prosper!"

All was silent. Lavrin and Calix worriedly glanced at each other, wondering what would happen. Not a sound came from their three captors. It was as if time had frozen.

Finally, a man walked up so close to them that they could hear him breathe. "Speaking the King's motto doesn't prove you are innocent." The man stared at them coldly.

"Stop, Felloni, you are making it harder than it needs to be," Chan replied. "We will know if they are telling the truth soon enough. If they really serve the King, they are just like us."

"Tell me, since when do the followers of the King tie up men for no reason? If you also follow the King, then you will know that what you are doing to us is wrong. Give us a chance to explain ourselves, please," Lavrin asked.

Chan motioned for the group to step away from Lavrin and Calix so they could speak alone. There was some back and forth negotiating and a couple of glances towards them. After a few minutes of discussion, Felloni began to second guess himself. He wondered if they really were followers of the King. It was possible.

When they returned, Chan said to Lavrin, "Go ahead, explain yourself."

29

Lavrin answered, "My friend Calix and I have both lost our parents, and have stuck together in the Forest of Bane. We hoped to train well enough to join the King's army one day. Until then, we decided to remain as rangers of the forest. We were at Saberlin to gather supplies when we saw one of you sneaking into an alleyway. We went to the abandoned house where we saw someone take the manuscripts from a woman there. We actually distracted some guards from following you. We could have allowed them to find you, but instead decided to let you go free. We followed you to discover what was going on. It was then that you ambushed us in the forest. We thank you for the wonderful hospitality you have shown us for what we did for you." Lavrin shook his head and rolled his eyes.

Felloni blushed; he had been the one who acquired the manuscripts while Chan and Grax had created the distraction. He could see now that he owed them the biggest apology. "I am sincerely sorry; we were trying to recover those manuscripts before Zekern discovered them. They contain vital information from the King."

The two were untied from their posts and brought to the Silent Watchers' secret treehouse. Before entering with the others, Chan met with a man from Ken Van, and handed the precious papers over to him. After the man left, Chan followed the rest of his group into the treehouse.

CHAPTER 3

NADRIAN

The tree house was well hidden. Someone could walk right on by and never know the home of the Silent Watchers was above their heads. The tree house was made up of three wooden huts connected by planks. Branches and vines were woven between most of the planks, allowing for a natural camouflage effect. Each hut had a straw roof and woven hammocks. The middle hut had a large table and a storage area for food. It also held a rope ladder which could be raised and lowered as needed. The two huts on either side were mostly for sleeping.

Inside, the group sat quietly at the broad table. Calix inspected the two other members of the group and could tell they were experienced fighters.

Grax was a large, bold warrior with thinning hair that didn't seem to fit his muscular body. He wore chain mail, boots and large gloves. He appeared incredibly strong, able to bust down any door. Several times he tried to lighten the mood by telling Lavrin and Calix about himself and asking them questions. He seemed very friendly to the newcomers, and they were glad he was open-minded.

Felloni, on the other hand, was a shy and often silent ranger. What he lacked in openness, he made up for in alertness. His hair was speckled with dirt, and scars ran across his arms. He had blackened his face so no one could clearly make out his appearance.

Chan had told them that Felloni would take time getting used to, but that he was an expert hunter. He could survive weeks in any circumstance and knew how to make due with little resources. No one knew why he was always pessimistic and quiet, and no one ventured to ask.

Lavrin and Calix learned how the Silent Watchers crossed the land, seeking ways to help the King. They had banded together out of their unified desire to see Natas' reign end. They had combined their resources and abilities to become a highly effective task force for the King.

Between assignments, they had trained and acquired resources from the forest. These would be used for trading with traveling merchants leaving Saberlin, especially ones favorable to the King. Occasionally, a couple of them had sought out employment in Saberlin, not so much for the money, as much as for the information that could be gathered there. Many alliances were formed during those work details. Although the work was hard, the Silent Watchers found great reward in helping the King.

"We should not have been so harsh to you," Chan said with regret. "We had found out that Zekern planned to burn these papers with the hope of blotting out Saberlin's foundation in the King's ways. It appears we could not see

33

past our mission to grant you the kindness you deserved. We can see that you have noble spirits and hearts. It is by the King's design that you followed us. I am glad you have discovered us before Zekern learned about your zeal for the King.

"We have become increasingly desperate as time has passed. Ever since Zekern has taken control of Saberlin, he has used his power to take out our forces. He has at least fifteen of our men serving him in his dungeons. Furthermore, his thugs are constantly on the lookout for our group. They have ruined more of our men than we care to mention. The four of us are the only ones still free."

Calix raised an eyebrow. "I only count three of you. Where is the fourth?"

"Our friend should be returning here shortly, and once we are all gathered together, we will convene to decide our next move," Chan answered. "Time is short, and I hope that with you two on our side, we will be able to do something about Natas' influence in the area. We have shed many tears and endured much hardship to get this far, and I will not let it go to waste."

Grax yawned. "It's late, let's rest; we all seem tired. I will be useless tomorrow if I don't get at least a few hours in."

"Grax is right. We need to rest for the night," Chan agreed. "Lavrin, you will sleep in the empty room. Felloni will take you there. Calix, would you mind sleeping on the floor? We do not have any other spare beds, but I can offer you an extra blanket."

"Yes, that will be fine," Calix sighed. "Lavrin and I have done that many times before."

The rustling of the leaves and the sound of the trees swaying back and forth like a tide echoed through the forest. An occasional owl could be heard, but in no time at all they were sound asleep. Their dreams were muddled and confused, overwhelmed by the massive amount of information they had just learned.

As everyone slept, the crickets nearby masked the night in a methodic rhythm. It was as if the forest held an anthem which it repeated all through the night.

Three hours later, before the sun had risen, Lavrin was awakened by a noise. "What are you doing here, traitor? You ruined my life once before, and I will not be so gracious to you this time." Lavrin opened his eyes to find a masked figure staring fiercely at him and pointing a long dagger just above his chest. He daringly rolled to his left, knocking his assailant to the floor. He got up and darted down the descending planks. His heart was pounding like a war drum, adrenaline surging through his body.

"What do you want from me?" Lavrin screamed as he fled from his pursuer down the stairs into the central hut. He then scrambled halfway down the ladder, jumped onto the ground and caught his breath, fumbling to draw one of his daggers. The rest of the group emerged from the center hut to see Lavrin collapse to the ground. The masked

35

warrior had blown a quick strike to his back from a spike which extended from a bow.

Lavrin crawled backwards as he tried to endure the pain of the thrashes. Chan quickly lit a torch, grabbed the attacker and whispered, "He's a friend, a follower like us." At that, the masked figure looked at Lavrin, now able to see who he truly was in the torch's light. Traces of blood tinted the nearby grass and bushes dark red. The attacker stood there dumbfounded as the others carried Lavrin up the ladder to tend to his wounds. As Chan stood over Lavrin's limp body, he was very afraid. Luckily, he could see the painful grimace on Lavrin's face, which indicated he was still among the living.

"Who is this person, and why hasn't he been tied up yet?" Calix asked. "He just attacked Lavrin."

Calix, confused and angry, was shocked to hear that this person was the last member of their group. How could a follower of the King be so cruel and rash? Another surprise came when he saw that it was a woman, not a man, standing over Lavrin. Her brown cloak was stained with fresh blood. She had two curved spikes attached to her bow, also stained with blood, and a dagger at her side.

Before long, they were all seated again at the table. Lavrin could barely sit upright with bandages across his torso. "Friends, I am sorry for the recent turn of events. Can we please straighten things out?" Chan proposed. He paused, and then continued. "We have before us two new friends. Lavrin and Calix, since you have met three of us, let us introduce the fourth. This is Nadrian. She has been with us from the beginning. She did not understand the situation. She takes threats very seriously and obviously mistook your intentions."

"I would like to ask forgiveness for my actions," Nadrian interrupted. "I was wrong to strike you. In the darkness, you looked like a man who had once betrayed me, robbed me and left me to die in the mountains. When you knocked me to the floor and ran off, I assumed you were him."

"I forgive you in full," Lavrin weakly answered. "I understand how you feel about protecting your friends. If I had felt my friends' lives were in danger, I would have done the same. Now I know not to get on your bad side in the future."

"I am glad you are so understanding and can forgive our friend," Grax said, clearly relieved. "She may be impulsive, but she can wield the bow like none other and has the reflexes of a panther. The time will come for us to explain things further, right now we need to plan our next mission."

"You are right, Grax, we do need to discuss this. However, let's give Nadrian and Lavrin some time to rest," Chan answered. They adjourned their meeting, and after several hours of sleep, Lavrin and Nadrian were well-rested. Although Lavrin was still frail, the pain of his wounds had subsided. There was no way to know for sure how long it would take for him to recover, but Lavrin felt as though the King was aiding him and healing his inflictions.

Meanwhile, Calix and the others patrolled the surrounding forest and hunted for food. Luck was with them; they stumbled across a six point deer grazing near a water spring. It was only a twenty minute walk from the tree house. Calix watched as Felloni masterfully crept up to a fallen tree and, drawing a long throwing knife, launched it right between two trees and into the neck of the deer, causing it to stumble forward and fall not ten steps from where it was hit. Only an expert could have made such a shot. They would be eating well today.

In the afternoon, Lavrin and Nadrian gathered with the others for a midday meal, which consisted of freshly acquired venison, porridge and fruit. Chan and Nadrian whispered to each other during the meal. Nadrian relayed all of the information she had acquired on her mission. She had been tracking a group of traders out of Srayo. Chan had a grim look on his face as he ate. Everyone clearly recognized he was distraught. Something was not as it should be. Nadrian finished her report; she believed those merchants were stealing from the people. Chan bit his lip. He had been hoping those traders would be allies to their cause.

"I hope you are good with a weapon. Things may get chaotic while you are with us," Felloni whispered to Calix.

"I've been practicing with this sword for the last five years. I would wager I could give any man a fight."

When he had finished his meal, Chan cleared the empty bowls and set a map on the table. "Let's begin," Grax urged.

"Be calm, Grax," Chan answered. "We must inform Nadrian and Lavrin of the plan." Chan, Grax, Calix and Felloni had been preparing and discussing plans throughout the morning, and they had devised a strategy before the other two had woken. They had decided to travel to the town of Dreylon. At Dreylon they would replenish their supplies and hopefully gain intelligence on Zekern's henchmen. When Lavrin and Nadrian heard the plan, they agreed. They hoped to put the recent events behind them.

CHAPTER 4

DREYLON

Waking up early the next morning, they started on the long trip toward Dreylon. Passing thorny thickets and muddy paths, the team crossed the eastern end of the Forest of Torin. This trip would be treacherous for most. Most people traveled the main roads where the way was easier, but for the Silent Watchers, there were too many thugs patrolling the roads - these kind of encounters they could do without.

The Forest of Torin was known as the hidden land to many townsfolk. The trees in the forest grew so tall and so thick that the forest often felt like a cave. Sometimes, rays of light passed through the trees, but at other times, so little light actually made it through that a torch was needed during the day. Of course, this caused many who ventured into it to feel frightened. Rumors of curses and evil creatures kept the forest free of unwanted guests. The Silent Watchers used the forest to their advantage to move freely through the region without Zekern knowing their whereabouts.

Taking advantage of the three day journey, the team used the time to get know each other better. Chan talked about his childhood on the Island of Hessington, named after Lord Hessington who had founded the settlement. The Island of Hessington was pastureland from coast to coast.

The farmers let their cattle roam and their sheep wander freely. The boundaries of each family's land were known well by all who tended the flocks, but if they were crossed, no one bickered about it. It was a simple place, but its people were loyal. Each house had the King's emblem displayed for all to see, and each man helped his neighbor during both the bountiful and the harsh times. Chan had spent many afternoons sitting with his friends on the rolling hills, watching the clouds take shape. He milked the cows for his father, and when he was older, he went into town to trade for whatever his family needed.

On his third trip to town, he heard the townsfolk mumbling about black-sailed ships that would cross every so often near the island. A few days later, Chan saw a ship dock in the harbor. He rushed to his village and warned his parents, who in turn warned the rest of the town. The villagers throughout the island gathered arms. The soldiers who disembarked were soon followed by two other ships carrying soldiers. The battles that ensued were gruesome, and many homes were burned to the ground. When the soldiers from the King arrived, the invaders retreated, for they knew they did not have the numbers or the supplies to take the rest of the island. The survivors praised the King for saving them, for without His soldiers, they would have been completely vanquished. From that day forward, Chan had sworn to go to the mainland and help others fight against the savage work of Natas. He could not sit by and watch what happened to his home happen to others across Amcronos. When he eventually reached the mainland, he decided to head northeast, down a river heading inland.

Nadrian had lived in the northwest part of the desert region. There were four tribes in the desert: the Bactran, the Helix, the Sadron and the Ioga. Nadrian was from the smallest tribe, the Sadron. She learned the duties of a young Sadron girl quickly. She would wash the laundry, cook when necessary, sew clothes and follow her father's orders when given. This life bored her, however; she had soon memorized the daily routine of the town and when trading was most busy. One day, she saw a large group of traders come in to town.

"Although I had always longed to be free from the Sadron, it was incredibly hard for me to leave my family," Nadrian told the group. "They were the one thing that almost kept me from leaving. Yet when I saw the traders enter our camp, I saw my opportunity and ran away. I had done many things I was not proud of, and was facing banishment if I didn't comply with the rules of the tribe. I could not bear to see my family suffer such shame on my account.

"When I left, I headed north for days. Finally, after passing the mountains bordering the desert, I felt the cool breeze of the forest. I made it to the nearest city and there met Chan. Chan was the one who taught me about the King. I owe him my life for bringing me out of my darkness to the King's light. Following the King has changed me from being a self-serving person to someone with a great purpose for my life. I will never go back to how I was before."

Nadrian and Chan had decided the Forest of Torin would be a suitable place to live. They had heard that while it was somewhat isolate, it was also close to many towns which followed the King. They hired a ranger to lead them north through the forest and help them build a shelter. This ranger, Felloni, knew many things about the forest and its creatures. He and his father were expert hunters, always scavenging the forest and tracking down all sorts of animals. The forest was hard to adapt to for those who had lived in pasturelands and deserts, so Felloni had to show them how to hunt and track. He went to Dreylon, where he sold his trappings to buy the necessary supplies to build them a tree house. Together, they wove ropes, cut down trees which they fashioned into planks, and made cloaks for Nadrian and Chan so they would blend into the forest.

The three learned which of the towns, cities and castles honored the King of Light and which were against him. They had found ways to help the King's messengers throughout the land. Felloni had planned to leave when the tree house was finished, but in the end decided to remain with them, adventuring through the land for the King of Light.

*****

As they ventured through the Forest of Torin, Nadrian decided to tell the story of one of their most exciting missions. They had been following a group of Natas' horsemen with some other rangers they had joined. When they had gone up into the mountains they split up, and the ranger leader, who Nadrian had gone with, betrayed her to the horsemen. These horsemen quickly captured and bound her. They had been carrying plans from Natas to Srayo, but now realized they were not alone. They doubled their speed, with Chan and Felloni following closely behind. If those horsemen reached the open plains, it would have been almost impossible to thwart them before they reached Srayo.

"Luckily, Chan and Felloni shot down a few of the horsemen while they descended the slope," Nadrian continued.

The remaining five had taken off into open grass. Chan and Felloni had jumped onto two of the now rider-less horses and took pursuit. The men were slowed by their prisoner, which allowed Chan and Felloni to catch up. Srayo was in sight. Chan knocked off a man with his sword but struggled to keep on his own horse. As the four evil knights entered Srayo, Chan and Felloni leaped past the guards, pursuing the knights through an alley. The knights then split, two going one direction with the plans, the other two with Nadrian. Chan bolted after Nadrian while Felloni barely dodged a rolling cart to continue chasing the knights with the plans.

Chan soon was next to the knights, but then something unexpected happened. The knight without Nadrian jumped onto Chan, tackling him to the ground. As the other knight rushed toward the lord's estate, an axe was suddenly thrown at him, hitting him in the chest. Unable to control the horse because of her bindings, Nadrian hit the ground. The horse galloped frantically about, then rushed out of the city. A man, large and strong, picked up the axe he had thrown and unbound Nadrian. He then rushed to Chan, picked up the enemy knight and tossed him aside as if a toy. As the big man raised his axe, the knight fled for his life. Chan went to thank the stranger, but then saw Felloni lying on a horse, blood rushing from his arm.

Nadrian bandaged his wounds as best as she could, and the four rushed out of town, hoping they were not followed. The large man said he had once been recruited into Natas' army, but had been captured in a battle on the northwestern shore of Lake Tibern. In the camp of his captors, Grax was amazed by the compassion the King's men had shown him. He told them all he knew of Natas' plans and, in the end, decided to join the King's men. He was welcomed joyfully and was assigned to infiltrate Srayo's barracks in order to take back some stolen weaponry.

He had seen the fight erupt in the alleyway. He could not stand by and watch the knights of Natas kill Nadrian. Grax had not been able to complete his mission, but had saved Nadrian's life, instead. This was how Grax had come to join them, and how they had become a group in service of the King.

*****

Arriving at Dreylon, the group knew they needed enough money to buy provisions. They were down to their last few copper coins, and needed enough supplies to last them at least a few weeks. They needed more than what the

46

forest could provide for this mission. Lavrin, Calix and Grax went east toward the market and the inner part of town, while Chan, Nadrian and Felloni went west, down a series of narrow roads.

The town was full of merchants trying to draw customers to their stores. Practically every business was having a special sale in order to compete with the other thriving stores. Too many people to count, both rich and poor, flocked around the town looking for the best merchandise.

Noises bombarded the scene. Chickens squawked, salesman shouted, customers bartered, feet stomped and doors rattled. It was almost too much for the forest dwellers to handle. They were used to the soft sounds and cool colors of nature. Now they found themselves in a crowded town with loud noises, bright colors and no freedom to move about. They were like peasants at a banquet or sailors on a mountainside.

After a few failed attempts to find some work, Lavrin, Calix and Grax entered the butcher's shop. There were a few slabs of meats being smoked in a large pit, and others salted and stacked for long-term storage. The skins were hung on ropes outside. Inside the shop, the trio was relieved to see no one except for the butcher. They finally got a moment of quiet.

The butcher was a broad man, with arms as thick as logs. He looked them over with his beady brown eyes as he walked up to the counter. "What can I help you with today?"

"Do you have any work for us?" Lavrin asked. "We are not from around here, as you can tell, and would like to earn some money."

The butcher looked them over again. They were at least wearing ranger's attire. He decided he could trust them. "A fine idea. As a matter of fact, I am in need of some help. You see, my regular deliveries have not come in because my son, who does most of the hunting, is sick. When I run out of meat later today, I will have nothing left to sell. Perhaps it is the King's blessing that you have made your way to my shop. Are you skilled in the hunt?"

"Yes, sir, we can catch just about anything: deer, boar, fowl… just about anything," said Calix.

"We will return as soon as possible," replied Grax, walking toward the doorway.

The butcher nodded and set their wages.

"I believe you two have this task well in hand," responded Lavrin. "Besides, three hunters will more than likely just scare the prey. I will look here in town for another opportunity. I will meet you at the large fountain we passed on the way here."

Grax and Calix returned to the forest in search of boar and deer. They were glad to get out of the town. They enjoyed each other's company, and the hours flew by as they bonded in friendship. Grax grew to admire Calix's bravery, and Calix grew fond of Grax's honesty and openness.

Lavrin, still sore from his wounds, looked for work at the nearby blacksmith's shop. His father had trained him from a young age in the art of crafting metal, in the hopes that Lavrin would take over his shop when he retired.

When he reached the blacksmith's, Lavrin recognized the hammer and anvil on its sign. He could tell this shop was much larger than the one he had been accustomed to. Lavrin never thought he would enter a blacksmith's shop again. Memories of his childhood flooded back to him as he walked through the door.

It was hot inside, but Lavrin embraced the heat and the clinking sound of metal with a smile. It reminded him of the times he would help his father when he was a lad. There were some swords and shields and other weapons on display. These were simple, because the blacksmith did not make weapons often. Most of the shop was filled with rakes, shovels and hoes for the nearby farmers. Blacksmiths had many different tools and many different techniques; it was a hard art to master.

"Fine stock you've got here. Any way I can help?" Lavrin asked.

"Can you straighten a plow, sharpen a scythe or light the fires?"

"Indeed, I can do it all, sir."

The blacksmith set the wages and Lavrin got to work. Working at the shop allowed him to rest his legs, and his arms felt up for the task. He kindled the fire and skillfully struck into the hard metal plow with ease. Lavrin and the blacksmith bonded over of their similar interests which kept the scene lively. Lavrin occasionally cringed from the pain of his wounds, but shrugged it off and continued working, knowing they needed the money.

******

Chan, Nadrian and Felloni were heading down a dirt path along some pastureland when a farmer called out to them. "Young travelers, could you spare a few hours to help me harvest my crops?"

"Of course," Felloni answered as they walked across the field. The farmer was old, yet was still strong enough to help them harvest the wheat. He had already completed part of the job, but did not have the strength to do the rest alone. Felloni and the others worked hard and soon were chopping their way toward the center. Sweat drenched their skin and their feet ached, yet they were used to the sting of a hard day's work. The bountiful harvest of wheat was long, golden and straight, and in the afternoon light it shined as gold shimmering in a lake.

"This is a large harvest you have this year. Where is your regular help? Surely you are not alone?" Chan asked the farmer who was straightening his straw hat.

"Unfortunately, I am alone. My wife passed away earlier this spring from a bad fever. My sons were both commandeered into service for Zekern in one of his mines to repay a debt we owed. I swear, if I was a younger man, the things I might do to that scoundrel," said the farmer.

"We are friends of the King. If there is any way we can help your sons, we will do it. I doubt we will be heading to the mines soon. I do know, however, that the King sees their plight," Nadrian said. Her heart broke for the families destroyed by Zekern's hand.

They worked with the farmer for the remainder of the day, telling him about the King's love as they went.

At the end of the day, the team gathered back in the marketplace, bought some food with their profits, and headed to the inn, where they rented two rooms. The rooms had little furnishings, but were inexpensive lodging for their stay in Dreylon.

Felloni, Nadrian and Chan carried in the food they had purchased while the rest counted the remaining money, which amounted to twenty silver and seven copper coins. "A decent earning for one day. We have worked hard. Well done, everyone," proclaimed Chan.

For a long while, the six talked about their encounters of the day and the jobs they had completed. Grax and Calix shared how they had almost plummeted face first into a stream while chasing a boar through the trees. Lavrin told the group about a conversation he had with one of the blacksmith's customers who had broken his axe on a stubborn oak tree.

Nadrian, Felloni and Chan talked about their time with the farmer harvesting the plentiful wheat. Chan recounted how he had chased off an entire flock of crows with his sickle as they tried to eat the wheat. "There must have been at least fifty of those pesky birds swarming around me."

Nadrian was quick to reply. "I only remember about ten, and they were not swarming around you at all. They took one glance at you and fled as fast as their wings could take them."

"All right, maybe I exaggerated just a little."

As they ate, Calix thought about his time with Lavrin in Saberlin. He thought about how much had changed in the once fair city. Would it ever return to its former glory? Suddenly, he remembered the warning they had received. "Lavrin, do you remember the woman in Saberlin who warned us?"

"Yes, I remember her. The mason's wife. What was it she said? Oh, that's right. She was telling us about Zekern's thugs who were due to arrive in the city."

Calix paused before continuing. "Do you think they have arrived there yet?"

"I doubt it."

Calix turned to Chan. "They might be the same thugs who have been attacking your band. If this is the same group, they are a threat that needs to be dealt with. If they are headed for Saberlin, they will likely take the trade route south through Dreylon or north through the mountain pass. If they return to Saberlin, it could mean real trouble. I think we should try to stop them. What do you think?"

"I think we definitely should," Chan said. "If these thieves reach Saberlin, they will spread havoc, and Zekern will force everyone to treat them like heroes. He will only grow stronger through the arrival of these brutes. The only problem is determining which route they will take. We could split up to cover both paths, but then we would be more vulnerable. If we stay here, however, we might miss them. We can't intercept them at Saberlin; Zekern's troops would overrun us. "

"It is not too far to the mountain pass. If we split up, we could come back together fast enough. That is, once we discover which route they are taking," Nadrian said.

"If they take the mountain pass, we can ambush them from the roadside," Grax added. "How I would love to pay back those cowards for what they did to us."

"So would I," Nadrian said. "Those heading for the mountain pass should leave early in the morning. If they have not passed us yet, then they will soon."

So after agreeing upon this change of plans, they went to sleep, weary from the day's work. Nevertheless, the thought of facing their new enemy remained with them, a storm cloud above their otherwise tranquil sleep.

******

Early the next morning, the sun awoke from its slumber and the sky glowed with beautiful tints of orange and purple. The group also awoke, and when they went outside, they felt the grass, wet from dew. Off in the distance a golden hawk was circling above, looking for his breakfast.

The group divided their supplies evenly, giving everyone enough to last. Nadrian, Chan and Calix left for the mountain pass, quickly striding through the plains. Lavrin, Grax and Felloni, however, headed toward the market to make use of the money they had left.

Grax carried the many purchases in his arms as he and Felloni walked up the broad staircase to their room. They did not realize that Lavrin had been pulled aside by a tall, well-dressed man who appeared to be rich and influential.

"Please spare me your time," the man insisted.

"I would like to return to my room, if you please." Lavrin turned to leave.

"I will not stop you, but I wanted to tell you that I'm hosting a gathering which many wealthy followers of the King will attend. It would be an honor to have you, and I believe many of my friends would be delighted if you came." The mysterious man gave him directions to his residence and slipped out the door, vanishing like a shadow.

Back at the room, Lavrin discussed the man's invitation with his friends, remembering his exact words.

54

Though at first they were unsure if this was a safe opportunity, the three decided that since this man was aware of their love of the King, he was probably trustworthy enough. At least they could attend the gathering and gain some needed information.

If the man was telling the truth, this was a chance they could not afford to miss. Maybe this was there chance to finally find some trustworthy allies outside of the group.

When they entered the rich man's estate that evening, they were surprised to see that the guests did not look wealthy like the man had said they would. The simple garments the men wore were the first sign they should have left the gathering. Instead they sat down at a table, against their better judgment. They noticed that many of the men had weapons at their sides, which was also suspicious. The three were met with dark glances, and a chill ran up their spines. They wondered where the "rich man" was that was supposedly hosting this meeting.

Lavrin knew followers of the King would not look at other followers with suspicion, but would be generous to them and greet them openly. Lavrin whispered his thoughts to Felloni and Grax. They felt the same way. Together, they got out of their seats and headed for the door. As they exited, everyone in the room swiftly drew their weapons and rushed upon them.

The rich man must have been a servant of Natas. Lavrin wondered how he had known to set a trap for them. The very thugs they had hoped to intercept had turned the tables on them, with more barbarians than they had expected.

Were the others safe? How could he alert them? These thoughts dominated Lavrin's mind. Then he remembered - the horn. He drew his horn and gave several loud blasts.

CHAPTER 5

SHOCK & LOSS

As he walked with Nadrian and Chan in the late evening, Calix sought out a suitable place to rest. They had been walking most of the day and were looking for a place to camp for the night. They had been delayed several times climbing the mountain pass. Finally, they found an open spot near some boulders. They set up their tents and prepared for the night. Calix, on guard, could hardly stay awake. It had been a three hour journey to reach the mountain pass, and they took rest along its side. Before they had left Dreylon, a signal had been established by the group. A series of three quick horn blasts meant danger or trouble. But for now, it was time to rest.

******

Chan and Nadrian quickly awoke. "What is it?" Nadrian asked.

Calix paced about anxiously. "I heard the horn in the distance."

"Was it three quick blasts?"

"Yes. We need to move down the mountain."

No more questions were asked. With all their speed they rushed toward Dreylon. Even though he was the most tired, Calix was the quickest runner in the group. He began to break ahead of his friends. Still, he wondered if they were going to be too late.

******

As they were trying to escape to the mountain pass, Grax, Lavrin and Felloni were cut off. Their enemies stared at them, ready to strike. Grax was a mighty warrior at heart, Lavrin knew, and Felloni had much skill with his knives. Still, chances were greatly against them. They realized that the mercenaries were more harsh and well-equipped than they had expected; they outnumbered the lone three ten-to-one. To make matters worse, enemy reinforcements were probably on their way.

"Odds look rough," Lavrin pointed out under his breath. "I wonder if the others are coming."

"So do I, but it's not likely at this point. They're probably finding a hiding place on the mountain pass by now. We have to get away from these people. If we can escape, we might be able to outrun them," Felloni whispered back.

"It is too late for that; besides, if the others do come, they will need our help. They'll be walking right into a trap."

"Agreed," the other two said. Followers of the King preferred non-violence, but they were also ready to use their weapons when necessary. Lavrin's hand went to his sword; he also possessed a dagger and a walking stick (not often used as a weapon). Felloni carried six knives which he could throw with precision, and two hand shields that extended to a spike. Grax was armed with two long axes and two long hammers. Fortunately, they had their weapons. They had almost decided to hide them outside the estate because they did not want to appear armed. However, today they were justified in the principle of keeping their arms close at all times.

"Well, what do we have here, a band of freedom fighters? I expected more of a challenge." Their leader laughed heartily. He was tall and the best looking and best fed of the group.

The three faced a trained, experienced force of wild slaughterers who were paid through plunder. Lavrin knew a fight with them would be no ordinary battle; it would potentially be the fiercest battle they had ever faced...and possibly the end of their lives.

The leader gave them one last chance. "Come with us, or die - your decision." When the commander saw them draw their weapons, he shook his head in disgust. "Kill them," he yelled to his band.

The swarm of mercenaries quickly surrounded the three, and charged at them with blood-lust in their eyes. Mercenary archers drew their menacing black bows and waited for the signal.

"The great King of Light, may he live and reign forever, and may his followers prosper!" Grax yelled. Lavrin blew his horn three quick blasts for the second time.

******

Calix, Chan and Nadrian were still edging their way toward the sound of the first horn blast. They ran with a renewed desire to save their comrades when they heard the second horn series. Something had gone terribly wrong.

"We must be cautious. Lavrin wouldn't keep blowing the horn unless they were in serious danger," said Calix as they ran down the slope.

******

Ting! Clash! Grax's weapons locked with a sword headed for his chest. Grax pushed his opponent off his feet and engaged two more within an instant.

Felloni braced himself as an enemy charged straight toward him. Felloni blocked the oncoming spear and jabbed his knife into the attacker's leg. He then was forced backward by several assailants.

Lavrin struck down the man Grax had thrown to the ground, and disarmed an oncoming warrior with a quick thrust of his sword. He threw his dagger at an archer aiming at Felloni before an onslaught of thrashes and strikes came upon him. He barely kept his footing as the impact pounded against him. He could not block many more attacks like that.

The three lost much ground and were forced into a back-to-back-to-back triangle formation. Lavrin wielded his sword with ease, keeping all who came against him on the defensive. Felloni, with only one extra knife, barely dodged the oncoming arrows. Grax crushed a helmet with his hammer but was stabbed in the leg with a spear. He felt the pain rush through his leg and was almost overpowered. The team survived the oncoming attacks, but knew they couldn't last much longer. As dark clouds rolled in, rain started to pour down, and the sun's light was blotted out like a blindfold. Lavrin and his friends kept fighting, clinging to their hope in the King.

A well-placed mace knocked Lavrin out cold, and the others tried to recover him in vain. They were too preoccupied with their own survival. Grax knocked down an archer and slashed his axes in rage. Grabbed by a few assailants, Lavrin was bound and thrown on a cart. He tried to open his eyes, but the pain was too great.

The monsoon flooded down, and the men struggled to keep their balance. Felloni parried and thrashed the oncoming warriors who were slipping in the mud. Grax charged an enemy archer and sent him reeling. Grax suddenly realized his mistake as he found himself separated from Felloni. Together, they could protect each other; on their own, they could be attacked from any angle. With Lavrin already captured, Grax feared that he and Felloni would not last much longer.

All of a sudden, Chan, Calix, and Nadrian charged into the battle, eager to help the team, and took the thugs by surprise. Renewed with hope, Grax soon reached the others, but was very hurt and could barely fight. Wild swings of his axe were about all he could muster. Chan could hardly recognize Grax through the downpour, and rushed to free Felloni from his fate. Nadrian's quick shots from her bow gained Felloni enough time to escape. The five saw enemy reinforcements and retreated from the battle, literally running for their lives.

They sped back toward the mountain pass. Felloni and Grax had to be helped along, but managed to continue onward. The trees that lined the mountains would have made a perfect cover, but the mercenaries were hot on their trail. Diving into the forest, Nadrian put a hand over Grax's mouth as he tried to scream out in pain. Luckily, the mercenaries decided not to risk fighting in the forest in this type of weather, where they could be shot by unforeseen arrows. They let their prey go, content with the damage they had done.

CHAPTER 6

HOPE FROM THE KING

About an hour had passed before the friends gathered enough strength to take shelter in a thick grove besides several fallen trees. After they were sure the bandits were not in pursuit, they turned their attention to each other. They were deeply bruised and worn out mentally and physically. After Nadrian removed her battered gloves, she stumbled up from the ground, then walked toward Felloni. He was resting, but had a look on his face of terror and dread. By the way he was shaking, Nadrian could tell he was reliving the battle in his sleep. She knelt down beside him, and examined his wounds.

Nadrian shook her head sadly. "Felloni's wounds are bloody, but luckily not deep." She looked at a cut in his side. She shuddered at the sight and quickly bandaged it with a roll of linen. It was not the cleanest covering, but it did the job. Nadrian tried to fix it, but her vision was cloudy from her falling tears. Suddenly, Felloni opened his eyes and gasped for air as if someone was choking him. Nadrian flashed into action, trying to settle his nerves, but she could not.

He rolled to his side and grappled for his dagger, but could not find it. Nadrian grabbed him by his shoulder and demanded, "Snap out of it, Felloni. We need you to stay calm."

"I need my knife," Felloni firmly answered. He grabbed Nadrian's arm. "Give me something to bite down on. The pain is unbearable."

Nadrian handed him a spare rag, and he chomped down on it like a dog. Felloni clinched his eyes tightly and laid as still as he could. Nadrian was about to continue bandaging his wounds, but heard a rustle in the bushes. She jumped to her feet.

She instantly regretted this decision, as pain shot up her leg. In reality, the noise was nothing but a few forest animals. She turned toward Chan. "We cannot stay here. Those thugs could be following us. They could be upon us any minute. They could be right on our trail. What if they are watching us? We need to move farther into the forest."

"No, Nadrian," Chan said. "There is no possible way we could move again. Felloni is reeling in pain, and I should be tending to Grax before his wounds become infected. You need to calm yourself, for all our sakes."

Grax's leg needed immediate attention, and Chan dressed it with some cloth doused in what little medicine they had. He laid a blanket over the tough, seasoned warrior, then laid back on a nearby tree.

Having dealt with the immediate medical issues, Chan dressed an arrow wound on his arm. "It's amazing how just a piece of wood with a tip of steel can cause so much harm. I would rather be attacked by a falcon."

Nadrian and Chan were about to say something to Calix, but decided to leave him alone as he sat with his head in his hands. They could tell he was distraught, and knew there was little they could do for him.

"We should hunt that group down," Nadrian said with clenched fist. "Lavrin needs our help. I owe him for how badly I treated him back at the treehouse. We may reach them if we hurry."

Chan turned toward her with eyes as piercing as knives. "I wouldn't last ten steps before collapsing. I'm glad you aren't injured, but I felt my life hanging in the balance during that fight. Luckily, we made it through... this time. But death will claim us quickly if we're not careful."

"Don't say such a thing. We've known each other too long and traveled too far to give up now. Maybe I can ask Calix."

"Please don't disturb him. I can tell by the pain in his eyes that his sorrows will take more time to heal than our wounds. Your zeal is great, Nadrian, and few could challenge you with the bow, but you cannot take them alone. Don't go. You are needed here to keep the rest of us alive."

Grax woke from his slumber. He roared in agony, instantly shocking the others. His knee flared with pain, and it would be at least a day until he could walk. There were still spots of dried blood speckled about his face from the fierce battle.

Unlike the others, Calix did not rush to help Grax. Calix sat alone, his head down, deep in thought. He felt ashamed by his tears, so he hid his face from the rest of the group. Lavrin, his first true friend, who had never abandoned him or failed in times of trouble, had needed his help. But he had been too late. Now all he could do was pray to the King that Lavrin would be fine and would live long enough for Calix to regain what was lost.

As he tried to sit up, Grax asked, "Where is Lavrin?"

"He was taken by the bandits," Calix remarked, with a sorrowful glance. It was a gaze that would blot out the sun, but Grax did not blame him for it. He only lay his head back down. He felt crushed by a great burden as if buried by rocks. He wanted to sit up, but knew better than to try.

The team knew they were lucky to be alive. Injured and defeated, they had barely escaped the battle without casualties. Little did they know the King had helped them escape from the thugs, and Lavrin's capture was part of his plan. The King helped all creatures and humans who needed aid and who followed him. He knew each one's purpose in the grand scheme of life. He was a glorious ruler of the Haven Realm and always knew the right thing to do in every circumstance. He had saved them for a special purpose, one they themselves could not comprehend.

Laying in the undergrowth, battered and weak, the group knew they would eventually need to move on. They desperately desired to free Lavrin from the rogues. Plots for their next course of action began to develop.

Later that day, the five discussed what to do next over a meager meal of stew. The fire they lit was small. It reminded Calix that although the flame of their hope was small, if stoked properly, it could grow into a large fire once again.

"I don't think we can defeat the bandits on our own," Chan said.

"But where can we go for help?" Nadrian replied.

"Our list of allies has grown thin. We definitely cannot go to Saberlin. Even if the people of Saberlin remember the King, Zekern has barricaded the city with an overload of guards," Grax answered.

"I think we should return to our homes to restock and heal," Calix said. "That seems like our best option."

"That would be wise considering the state we're in. We are in no condition for another fight," Nadrian said.

"The rain has stopped, and I'm sure Natas' men will be looking for us soon. We must make our way deeper into the forest," Calix said.

"I agree," Grax replied.

The five companions were on their way within two hours. The trip back would be slower and more challenging due to their injuries, especially Grax's leg. Thankfully, the way would be free from thugs through the shaded tree line.

******

As they entered the plains north of the Forest of Bane, they saw the remains of a burned-down barn. The wreckage stood out clearly from the swaying grass which surrounded it. As Calix stepped over a fallen piece of fence, his boots met the ash. The group neared the barn, knowing they were far from the main road and thus far from danger. Chan placed his hand on his sword's hilt when he heard the neigh of horses. After he turned the corner of the barn, he saw a girl, covered in soot, helping a young boy onto a horse.

As the others rounded the corner, the girl turned and then stepped back. "Who are you? Stay back!" She drew a small knife and held it out toward Calix threateningly.

Calix unsheathed his sword and threw it aside on the charred ground. "We don't mean you any harm. How did you survive the fire?"

The boy, only about ten, wore a torn shirt and earth-toned trousers. "We were out in the forest picking berries when we saw smoke. We ran back home to find our house and barn were on fire. At least our horses broke out before the barn collapsed." He paused, then rubbed his eyes. "We don't know what caused it or where our father and mother are."

Calix suspected this was the work of Natas' minions, burning and pillaging as they had done to Lavrin's home years ago.

The blonde haired girl, about five years older than her redheaded brother, still seemed unsure of Calix's trustworthiness. She weighed her options, and decided they may need his help after all. Putting away the knife, she said, "Since all we have is gone, we should make our way to the refugee camp. We know some other families have been hiding out there."

Chan stepped toward them. "Do you know where the camp is? Perhaps we can take you there."

"It's in the Mud Ridge Valley somewhere. At least, that's what we heard from a family that passed through a couple of weeks ago. I don't exactly know where that is," she said. "We will go with you if we can, but we will take care of ourselves."

"Our path leads us in that direction," Chan answered. "We would be glad to help you find this camp. It must be hidden well, for I have passed the ridge many

69

times and have never seen a camp before. Have you, Calix?"

"No, I have not," Calix responded. "Yet, it's very possible that there is something hidden in the rugged landscape of that area."

Nadrian walked over to the children and helped them gather their things. She smiled at the boy, who innocently returned the gesture. The girl wore a tattered skirt and had freckles on her tear-stained face. Calix could tell she acted like a mother to her younger brother. "I'm Eli and my sister's name is Margret," the young boy said with a faint smile.

The two farm horses were a blessing to the newly enlarged team. Eli and Margret were set on the smaller horse while Grax rode the larger horse, since it was hard for him to walk on his injured leg. The group headed into the forest. They would stop by their tree house along the route to the camp. "We will eventually have to pass Xala Lake to get to the Mud Ridge Valley," Felloni said. "I hear it's dangerous and filled with rare, mysterious creatures."

"Is there a way around it?" Nadrian asked. "We wouldn't want to cross paths with anything that would give us a serious fight."

Felloni sighed. "No, I'm afraid not. Unless you want to steer a long distance off course, we will need to travel past it. Who knows if rumors are true, anyhow?"

"Hopefully, no wild animals will give us any trouble." Grax smiled. "But if they do, they had better watch out. I'm as hungry as a bear."

******

In the morning, the small troop continued through the Forest of Torin. At first they traveled at a brisk pace, however they soon slowed when they hit a flooded area.

"Ugh. A river overflowed, probably due to the spring rains." Grax descended toward it. Branches hung down everywhere. With water up to their knees, Calix, Chan and Nadrian followed him. Gnats swarmed around them, a constant bother.

Nevertheless, the seven, still true to the King, ventured through the forest with little sight of the sky. The leaves were growing back now that it was early spring, providing them shade from the ever-present heat.

Margret, although only fifteen, knew some things about medicine from her mother. She had Felloni's and Grax's wounds properly bandaged and, with Nadrian's help, she found enough herbs to make a poultice. This was applied to their wounds as they rested.

******

As they approached the familiar surroundings of their tree house, Felloni rushed ahead and lowered the rope ladder. They were glad to be back at the place they called home, even though they would not be there long. Eli was excited, seeing the tree house as an adventure to explore. He was awed by its wooden walkways and its huts nestled in the trees. As the others entered, Nadrian smiled at the sight, but Grax just collapsed on a hammock, exhausted. At first they all thought Grax was tired, but after further examination, Margret noticed he had caught a fever. She quickly ran for a wet cloth to help calm it.

After a week's time, the team had restocked their food, sharpened their weapons, and reenergized. Grax's and Felloni's wounds were healing, and Margret and Eli seemed to trust the group more. Grax was very relieved to be recovering from the fever.

Chan tended to their two horses and packed them down with supplies. Fortunately, they were bred to be strong. He treated them as if they were his own. It was the best way for Chan to take his mind off of his injuries. The time at the treehouse progressed slowly for everyone until the team was ready to continue their mission. They set out toward the Mud Ridge Valley as soon as Grax and Felloni were healthy enough to do so. Chan walked ahead, clearing paths for the horses. It would take another two days before they would reach Xala Lake. Felloni was aware that when they found the lake, they might encounter wild and unheard-of creatures. Inwardly, he hoped they would.

To pass the time, Grax decided to carve a wooden sword for Eli. It took him quite some time to complete, but he gave it to him an hour shy of reaching Xala Lake. The boy was thrilled to receive his gift. Grax had a new friend.

******

When they reached the broad Xala Lake, they saw its clear water had a slightly purple hue. Long silver fish swam on its floor. Chan wondered if the horses should be allowed to drink the water, afraid that it may be poisonous or magical.

"Since we are almost through the Forest of Torin, I think this would be a fine place to rest," said Calix.

The seven set up camp, but continued to scan the area, just in case. No sooner had they situated themselves when suddenly a roar was heard off to the right. The group rushed to the scene with weapons ready. They had no idea what they were getting themselves into.

Up on his hind legs, a leopard was battling a pack of fire hounds. The leopard wore leather armor with the King's emblem on the side. His claws were fully extended, and his eyes darted back and forth. He knew fire hounds were excellent killers. They looked like wolves surrounded by flames. Their bite was severe because of the fire in their teeth.

The team quickly joined the leopard's side, knowing anyone wearing the King's emblem was an ally. This sent the five hounds into a rage, lunging and biting with razor-edged teeth. Nadrian drew back her bow, and Chan brought out his sword. Suddenly, the blazing fire hounds charged the group.

One of the beasts sprang toward Grax and pounced onto his back. Grax would not tolerate this and wrestled the beast to the ground. Felloni stabbed a hound, sending him reeling, yet not killing him. The creature responded by diving at Felloni's legs, pinning him to the ground. Before the fire hound could bite him, Nadrian let loose an arrow into its side. It whimpered loudly, then fell.

The remaining fire hounds rallied against the team. Their eyes lit with a ghostly fire, and they surrounded their enemies like jackals. They attacked them with their flaming teeth from multiple directions, but it was to no avail. The group countered the beasts' assault with one of their own, which caught them off guard. Soon the hounds were beaten back by the group's efforts, either slammed by weapons or clawed by the leopard. They rocketed away, and the team did not wait for them to return.

The team gathered back at their camp, and made sure no one was seriously injured. Though Grax had mostly recovered, and Nadrian and Calix were not wounded, Chan and Felloni were not so lucky. Felloni had added to his wounds and felt miserable. Chan's arm had been bitten, which sent a sharp pain surging into his shoulder.

The group was glad that their two younger members had stayed at the camp and had not followed them toward the battle. Margret and Eli were shocked to see the leopard clothed in leather armor walking with the group.

"Thank you for assisting me. My name is Macrollo. I am a messenger from the Haven Realm," the leopard said.

"The King of Light instructed me to come to this forest and to find some of his followers. I need help reaching Hightenmore Castle. I pray you are the ones he told me about."

The group stood in utter shock, not knowing what to think. Had they fallen into some kind of dream?

After some time, Chan whispered a reply. "I have heard that the King can grant animals the ability to speak, but I never thought I would meet one who could."

Eli jumped up and down with excitement. "No one is ever going to believe this!"

"As to your question, brave leopard, we do follow the King. But we weren't expecting you," Chan said.

"Sometimes the King works in mysterious ways; he knows what already has happened and what will come to pass. I am amazed so few truly recognize him as King in these lands. It is a drastic difference from where I come from."

"We were on our way to a refugee camp in the Mud Ridge Valley," Calix said. "We have a friend who was captured by Zekern's men. We want to rescue him but we cannot do it alone. Do you think if we go to Hightenmore they will help us?"

"Of course. The men of Hightenmore always aid the King's followers. I know where the refugee camp is; there are many of the King's followers there. I will lead the way," Macrollo replied.

The group packed up and headed out of the area, following the leopard toward the edge of the forest and watching for the fire hounds' return. They set out for the Mud Ridge Valley with a new sense of purpose.

******

Along the way, Eli was filled with curiosity. He stared at the strange leopard for some time. "Are there others like you?" he asked. "Well, creatures like you, who can talk?"

Macrollo smiled. "Yes, in fact I once met a marvelous advisor of the King who was a hawk-like creature, as long as a man is tall. He had a silver body which was almost invisible in the sunlight. I've heard he is a master of stealth and can sling darts with precision. Truly at heart, though, he loves being the King's scribe."

"That's amazing. I wish I could meet him."

Macrollo looked at him as they walked. "Maybe someday you will, Eli."

Eli smiled at the thought and showed Macrollo his new wooden sword. Margret was glad that Eli was enjoying the ride so much. Nonetheless, she hoped they would reach the refugee camp quickly.

"What brought you to the Xala Lake?" Calix asked Macrollo.

"The King told me I couldn't reach Hightenmore without bringing a group of followers with me. I am fairly certain you are the ones I was sent to find. My journeys here have taught me to trust the King's hand in all things. I am one of the many messengers who delivers letters to his servants here. They are spread throughout the land, trying to diminish Natas' web of influence however possible."

"It's good to know we have allies out there," Calix replied.

"Yes. The King has far from forgotten Amcronos."

"You mention the King often. Have you actually seen him before?"

"No, I have not," Macrollo replied. "No one has, for you would die instantly if you beheld his infinite, blinding light. However, I have been in his presence before and have spoken to Him. He always knows the perfect words to say. Ever since I was a young cub, the King trained my parents to be guardians of his kingdom. They came here when the first colonies were founded. My mother and father battled against raiders who were hazing the newly established towns. They stopped many of them, but then died by their hands. I carry on their legacy under the King."

Calix placed his hand on Macrollo's shoulder. "I'm so sorry for you, Macrollo. My parents died of the plague many years ago. I am glad we came to your aid against those fiery menaces, and just in time, too."

The journey toward the valley was filled with lively conversation, and the group took into account everything Macrollo told them. They listened to every word he spoke, and discussed the ins and outs of the King's lands as they traveled toward the refugee camp.

CHAPTER 7

THE LONE LAVRIN

Lavrin had mixed feelings; he was afraid to be at the mercies of his captors, hopeful that he would be rescued, confused about what would be done to him, and quite frankly, hot and tired. To make matters worse, his head was pulsing with every step he took. His only reprieve was the limited sleep he could find when they stopped for the night. He was led through plains and hills, dragged along by force when his legs gave out. His body cried out for help, yet none was given. He was dragged by the soldiers most of the way, like prey being hauled away by its predator.

Finally, he saw a familiar yet disappointing sight: Saberlin. Its high stone walls brought no joy to his downcast eyes, and its waving banners brought disdain, not relief, to his soul. He was amazed how much he despised this place now, when he used to adore and admire it. How much the fair city had changed.

Lavrin knew that if he was not killed after his trial, he would be sent to work on Zekern's projects. He was not dismayed by the work, but by the thought that his comrades would be helping the King while he was in the pits. He earnestly wanted to be serving the cause, especially because of his father's passion for the King. Though his father probably now lay entombed in the ground somewhere, Lavrin wanted to make him proud. Ultimately, though, he realized who he most wanted to prove his devotion to was himself.

All his life he thought he needed to do more, to strive in the King's ways. Now all he could do was stagger along, guided by a coarse, large man like an ox to the butcher. Lavrin would have been appalled by the smell of his captors' moldy bread if he was not so hungry.

Whenever Lavrin stumbled to the ground, kicks, lashes and laughter beckoned him to get up. They jeered at him like he was less than human, like some stray dog in the streets. It would be a matter of time, but he was certain he would find a way to escape. Escape... escape was the rope his mind clung to in order not to fall off the mountain of despair.

Lavrin could tell little of what was happening, he was so confused and tired. His ropes were replaced with chains, and he was thrown into an empty cart which slowly pulled him toward Zekern's fortress. Lavrin knew Zekern did not like threatening forces and utterly despised the King of Light. Zekern considered himself supreme overlord of this region, although Natas was his ruler. He believed he had the right to make laws, and he never stopped amassing wealth. Though the people suffered, he did not care. He would rather see them crawl toward his throne than walk toward it.

Lavrin knew that although Zekern was powerful, he would eventually get in over his head, and the King of Light would judge him as he deserved. This was the fate that befell all arrogant dictators. Lavrin wished he could be with his companions; he wondered if he would ever see them again. Yet he knew that if he died, it would be the King's will to take him. Lavrin realized how much he truly longed for Vin, since he was one of his few reminders of his parents. Vin was his last memory of life before the fire. He vowed that if he ever saw his fuzzy terrier again, he would make sure he knew how much he loved him.

At the entrance of the castle grounds were two high towers that loomed like pillars of smoke. Large broad gates of iron opened slowly, beckoning him to his torture. The walls were stacked high with expertly cut stone, and filled in with plaster. The two donkeys pulled the prisoner through the gate. After entering, bags of loot were loaded on all sides of the cart, piling around Lavrin like boulders. After making their way toward Zekern's prison, the thugs unloaded him and took him into the tower on the right. Zekern's gold continued on toward the mansion.

Lavrin was sent through a decrepit door down into the dungeons where he was locked into a cell. There was little light, so for a while Lavrin just sat and let his eyes adjust. Moss covered the floor beneath him. The iron bars were rusted on all sides. Lavrin sat in a daze for quite some time, alone with his thoughts, until he noticed a young lady sitting at the other end of the cell. "Hello," Lavrin said, trying to gain her attention.

She turned around to see him. "Who are you?" she asked. She had red hair, pale skin and wore a tattered dress. Her expression was doubting, as if she was unsure if Lavrin would hurt her. She seemed like she had been abused regularly and was used to the sting of harsh words and fists. Lavrin looked toward the other cells, and noticed that they were empty, which surprised him. He expected Saberlin's jail to be overflowing with criminals. Lavrin supposed that no one was willing to stand against Zekern for fear of these dungeons.

After his eyes had fully adjusted, Lavrin started telling her about his past, starting with his meeting of Calix all the way to being captured. This took a few hours, but since it brightened the dark mood, he spared no details. She listened carefully, trying to tell if he was lying. When he asked her who she was and why she was brought here, she simply replied, "I would rather not say."

Lavrin eventually learned that her name was Kyra. After further conversation, she revealed that she had grown up as a child of wealthy parents who were followers of Natas and had given her to be one of Zekern's maidens. She

82

was brought to the dungeons after she tried to escape several times. She would be free to leave the dungeon if she agreed to behave. In reality, she preferred being imprisoned over Zekern's abusive behavior.

As the two bonded in undivided attention and complete friendship, Kyra was saddened by Lavrin's story and realized that she was not as bad off as she had once thought. Her parents were still alive, and she had never needed to scavenge a forest to find a day's food.

Lavrin went on to share with Kyra how at a young age he had chosen to follow the King. He talked of how the King dwells in the Haven Realm and has messengers who travel across Amcronos, sharing the truth of his kingdom and his goodness. It was one of these messengers, a knight travelling through Lavrin's hometown, who shared the truth of the King with him many years ago. Lavrin explained how Natas despised the King of Light because of his thirst for power and because of his pride. Most of all, Natas hated the fact that the King's subjects loved him, for no one had ever followed Natas out of love - only out of fear. Lavrin told her that the way to the King was found in surrendering one's own will to instead live for his purposes.

Kyra thought over each word; if the King of Light was this loving, why had she never heard of him before? "So, if I turn my heart to the King and pledge to follow his ways, he will love and guide me, and lead me to the Haven Realm?" she asked.

"Yes," Lavrin replied. "It may seem like the King would never hear a young maiden locked away in a dungeon, but his spirit fills the whole land. He will know."

She looked through the small barred window, up into the sky. "Great King of Light, I do not deserve this free gift you have bestowed on me. I wish to follow you so that your name may be known." Tears slowly filled her eyes. "I feel like I've never felt before. I feel... I feel free, like a bird that has finally learned to fly. When it spreads its wings and soars, it forgets all the trouble it took to get there. I can almost feel the light of the King with us here."

******

After a day, it was time for Lavrin's trial. While he was being taken by the guards to Zekern, Kyra whispered, "May the King be with you." Lavrin ascended the high stairs out of the dungeon and crossed the courtyard to the Great Hall where meetings were held.

Zekern was seated between his favorite wife and his highest advisor. His throne was scarlet and gold, encrusted with gems. When entering the hall up a high marble staircase, Lavrin spied rich tapestry hanging on the walls and gold artifacts which Zekern had recently received as gifts. This impressed Lavrin little; he assumed that the heavy taxes Zekern issued and his thugs' many raids brought these riches to him. The guards near Zekern wore black armor and stood at attention like statues. Zekern's advisor, seated to his right, was a plump man with an arrogant posture. He wore a fancy red coat and had a thick, twisted mustache. This advisor stared at Lavrin and frowned upon his unkempt appearance.

Zekern's wife wore a silver dress and had a golden pendant around her neck. She looked at Lavrin with intrigue, wondering how he had fought off Zekern's thugs, even if only for a moment. Lavrin, on the other hand, asked himself how any woman could love a villain like Zekern.

Zekern was clad in a dark suit of armor. It was finely detailed and engraved with dragons and tigers, showing his superiority. He wore a crown adorned with rubies and emeralds. Lavrin knew Zekern had no right to wear a crown - there was only one who held that right.

The guards encircled Lavrin, and he stared back at them through their faceplates. Their menacing appearance made them look heartless, as if they had no sympathy for the beaten Lavrin.

Zekern had heard the accusations and knew he could not let Lavrin go; he wanted to make an example out of him. So he talked with his advisor and decided on a suitable and substantial punishment to test his devotion to the King.

"So you are Lavrin, the prisoner I've heard so much about."

"Yes, I am Lavrin. I must admit you have turned Saberlin into a den of lions and tigers. It once was an amazing place; now I would rather be thrown into the ocean than live here."

"Well, drowning you is still a possibility," Zekern replied. "Yet, I think I will work you before I end your life. Where are your friends? The ones who so nobly fought against my soldiers?"

Lavrin clenched his fist. "They must have escaped your grasp. I thought no one could best you. I may work for you, but free Kyra, and I will strive even harder."

Zekern allowed a smile, seeing Lavrin's compassion had gotten the better of him. Zekern knew he could use this weakness. "Why should I set her free? She has betrayed me on numerous occasions. I would rather whip you."

"Personally, I would rather have a willing worker than one who would toil half-heartedly under your abuse."

Zekern changed the topic. "I have an arena which holds weekly entertainment for my citizens. They really do enjoy it. You will see it soon enough. You'll be one of the warriors, however, not a part of the crowd. I hope your skill in battle was not exaggerated, or my champion shall make quick work of you. If you manage to live, you shall remain a slave to me as long as I would like."

Being led away from the richly adorned lord brought satisfaction to Lavrin. He realized that he was blessed to be fighting in the arena, since it was a place where he could use his talents and skills to his advantage. It would just like the duels he had once had with Calix.

Lavrin used to tell himself that he was just an ordinary young man, trying to make his mark in a constantly shifting and changing world. Now he faced the fact that he was far from ordinary. In truth, his adventures and lifestyle were incredibly far from that of an ordinary man. If normality was a man, they had never been introduced.

The average man would not have lost both parents at such a young age, have chosen to live in the forest, have a friend quite like Calix Windrider, or have been interrogated by a group of rangers. Would anyone train themselves with the sword, then battle against sinister brutes following a tyrannical overlord? How many people were about to face a champion in a packed arena?

Lavrin stepped down the circular stairwell, forced onward toward his cell. He smiled a smile he had not shown for a long time. With eyebrows raised, he said to himself, "What has become of my life?"

CHAPTER 8

RUMORS

Lavrin had overheard the guards whispering that he was to be weakened for the event, so whoever he faced could easily defeat him. He was lucky the guards had been very open in their discussion of the upcoming battle. Lavrin knew he needed a plan to maintain enough energy to stand a chance against his foe.

Composure. Composure was key. Though Lavrin did not know who his opponent would be, he knew he would need all his power to defeat him. He decided that the best way to retain his strength was to take the path of least resistance.

It would not be an easy task. Taking mockery from the guards, performing whatever cruel tasks they assigned, and watching other slaves suffer would tear at his very heart. But Lavrin decided that small words of encouragement would do more good for the prisoners than an uprising ever could. One man could not change the course of an entire city without first changing his own course. This would be hard, almost impossible, but Lavrin knew he would get his chance soon enough. First the duel in the arena, then finding a way to defeat Zekern.

Sitting in his dark hole of a prison cell, Lavrin wondered if he was to be sent to the workforce or left to wait. Kyra had been summoned to spend the day slaving for their cruel masters, but Lavrin knew with him they would offer no mercy. As he was thinking through his plan of survival, he heard a humming noise. Turning around, he noticed a hole at the back of his cell which he had not seen before.

Restricted by his chains, Lavrin inched his way toward it. He made it to the hole after some effort and whispered, "That's a beautiful song."

The song stopped, and the other prisoner looked into the hole. From what Lavrin could see, he was an older man. His eyes were green, but looked tired and weary. "So, what has brought you here?" he asked Lavrin. "This dungeon usually does not attract people like you. Unless you are trying to butter me up for something."

"No, sir. I was only trying to be considerate. It really was a wonderful song. My friend Calix whistles all the time. I guess you reminded me of him. My name is

Lavrin. I was taken here because I fought against Zekern's rogues."

"Why would you ever fight against Zekern's henchmen? They are strong and ruthless. Most people just salvage what they can after their wreckage and move on with their lives."

Lavrin leaned in closer. "Because someone needs to stand up to the tyranny of Zekern's rule. I have allies who are trying to do this, as well. They escaped the battle. I remember the days of Zekern's father when Saberlin was a spacious, thriving city. Now it is on the path to ruin."

"I know as much as anyone where Saberlin is headed. I was put here because I was helping smuggle books of the King out of Saberlin. I kept them hidden until a ranger was able to get them out of the city. He escaped with the help of his friends, but I was not so lucky."

Lavrin sat back in awe. Could the man be referring to the exact same moment when he had met Felloni, Chan and Grax? "Meeting you here is no coincidence. When I told you I have allies who are serving the King, I first met them when they were taking manuscripts out of Saberlin. They are rangers, as well. We must have both been there at the exact same time."

Before the conversation could continue, Lavrin heard guards entering his cell. "Up on your feet, worm. Follow us if you want to keep your life." Lavrin obeyed and was dragged out of his confinement. The three guards forced him up out of the dungeon into the blinding light.

He looked across the market and saw struggling peasants following a group of merchants, hoping they would drop a morsel of food or some coins. Lavrin's heart was broken as downcast eyes watched him being dragged away.

Passing guards looked at him in judgment, then continued on their rounds. If only they knew what was really happening. If only they knew they were on the wrong side of this fight. Lavrin closed his eyes. If he could get out of Saberlin, he promised himself that he would do whatever it took to see people freed from the trickery of Natas.

Lavrin watched a triad of guards drag a man, dirty and bloodied, behind a building. Lavrin feared that this was the man he had met in his cell. Without any sound of struggle, the guards returned without the prisoner. Lavrin knew what they had done. He had hardly gotten to know the man, but he was empowered, not dismayed, by his sacrifice. He was fighting to save men like that, men who served the King no matter the cost. Lavrin only hoped he would not die in Zekern's arena before he was freed from his captivity.

Next thing he knew, he was shoved into Saberlin's barracks. Mud clung to the entryway, and dust covered every part of the room. Furniture lay in heaps on the floor. At least it was a darkened room, which eased his burning eyes.

"Clean it." The guard spat on the floor then turned away. The door was bolted shut behind him.

Standing on the far side of the room were five muscular men with grimaces on their faces. Lavrin felt chills run down his spine; they were some of the brutes he and his friends had fought against. Lavrin knew he would not get much cleaning done.

Trying to avoid eye contact, Lavrin bent down and grabbed the wooden bucket full of soapy water. He dipped the coarse brush into it and started scrubbing the dirty stone floor.

He heard footsteps walking toward him. Should he try to defend himself? No, stick to the plan. He would not take measures to the extreme. He would focus on the blessings of the King, not on the pain he knew was coming.

The rogues drew close to Lavrin, making him feel very small. They formed a circle around him, and he knew something horrible was soon to come.

For a short time, they stood above him, watching him scrub away the dirt and mold. It was unnervingly silent. Lavrin wanted to escape their piercing eyes, which he could fell digging into him as if they were searching his soul. But Lavrin thought of Kyra and the man he had met in the dungeon. Calix was out there somewhere too, if only he could see him again.

Lavrin made up his mind. His friends, especially Calix, would make the best of a situation like this. They would stand strong against any threat because of their love of the King.

The peace of the King overcame anything these brutes could do to him. It was stronger than even the haughty will of death. Lavrin knew death would not be claiming him this day, because Zekern had plans for him in the arena.

When Lavrin finished his thought, he felt screaming pain shoot up his leg. He looked up to see the thug on his right kicking him. Suddenly, an onslaught of punches and kicks engulfed him. His entire body screamed out in pain. He could not defend himself even if he wanted to.

After what seemed like an eternity, the beating ceased. The jeering laughter of the brutes ended, and the hard strikes no longer slammed into his side.

Lavrin slowly studied his wounds. He tried to get up, but his body refused. The hurt was far too great. Zekern had succeeded in wounding him before his match. Maybe he should have fought back after all.

In fear, Lavrin looked around to see if they were still there. They were gone. That was a glimmer of hope. Lavrin realized that if a guard was to come in and see him lying there, he would be punished. Zekern might even be sending guards to him this very instant. In order to avoid more pain, Lavrin rose and hobbled toward the pile of chairs.

One at a time, through gasping breaths, Lavrin placed chairs at tables and organized the area. He tried as hard as he could to clean up the barracks. He scrubbed until his bloodied arms ached. The barracks finally started to look clean, but there was still so much work left to be done. How could he fight after being so beaten?

He needed rest. He needed something to get himself mentally and physically ready for the disconcerting fate that was to come.

Weariness overtook his body, and he collapsed onto the hard ground. He was frustrated with himself. How could he give up? How could he not stand for the King? How could the King not stand up for him?

At that moment, Lavrin figured out something that would stay with him for the rest of his life: the King is always watching over his servants. He knows where his followers need to be and places them according to his plan. Somehow he was supposed to be in Saberlin. Somehow he would honor the King as an abandoned prisoner. But he was not abandoned…he was never abandoned.

CHAPTER 9

TOUGH DECISIONS

Zekern had decided that since Lavrin was a rebel fighting for the King's cause, his skill might provide some entertainment for his citizens. Lavrin would fight the top-ranking duelist in Zekern's newest arena built by his sizeable slave force. Zekern wanted him to suffer for his beliefs. They would battle until Lavrin rejected the King or died. Secretly, Zekern wanted Lavrin to do well enough to interest the crowds. As far as he was concerned, he could die after that.

Lavrin was tossed back into the dungeon cell, and the guard locked the door. "I'll be watching your fight." He sneered at Lavrin, then walked away.

Kyra, who had also been returned to the cell, gazed at Lavrin as he got up. "Lavrin, you look terrible. What happened to you out there?"

He wiped some dirt off his face. "My test has been decided. I am to go to the arena and fight Zekern's champion."

"That will be tough. I have watched those battles before. The champion has thick armor, but he's weak in the back. You'll be given a choice between a few different weapons. The shield will do little against his strength. He's merciless and charges furiously at his opponents. You'll want to stay light and use longer weapons."

"I did not take you for someone who partakes in such brutal events."

She paused. "I really only watched the first few minutes. I left as soon as I could. All I know is what the guards say. They seem to talk about the fights any chance they get."

Lavrin lay down and tried to get some rest; tomorrow would be a very tough battle. As he drifted to sleep, he thought of the days when he and Vin would sleep under the stars in the wet grass, and Vin would lick his face. What a different time and place he was in now.

******

Vin jumped down to the ground and barked loudly. No reply. He barked again. Still no reply. He knew something was wrong.

The scent of his owners was barely noticeable any longer. He was a hunting dog, however. He could track a scent for miles. It was his skill - sniffing out lost items was his specialty. Nose to the ground, Vin twisted and turned and eventually started in a northeastern direction. "Of course," he thought to himself, "they cannot be too far off. I will catch up to them soon enough."

Bolting at full speed, Vin searched for Lavrin and Calix, heading toward Saberlin. When he reached a stream, he saw a group of circling fish, daring him to take the plunge.

He had had enough with animals taunting him. He took the plunge into the cool waters. He pounced back and forth, trying to sink his claws into the slippery scales. Triumphantly, Vin ate the fish he had caught, then continued on in the same direction. Sadly, however, he had lost the scent. As the end of the forest came into sight, Vin rushed toward the bright sunlight into the open grassland. He turned north, and with his tongue and ears flopping in the breeze, ran with haste toward the shimmering city in the distance. Maybe he would find Lavrin there. Maybe he would find his master.

******

Lavrin entered the arena. He could hear the crowds cheering, ready for the bloody fight. This saddened him - so many people looking forward to death. He spied Zekern seated under a large overhead covering, surrounded by his advisors. The section in which they sat was far more glamorous than the common seating, as was to be expected.

Lavrin meditated on all that he was fighting for. He had to succeed – fighting for the King and for his friends was the only thing that mattered. He had lost all other motivation. This passion drove him onward, and that was all he needed.

The arena was oval shaped, but not exceedingly large. The ground was dry and dusty. Although the ground was uneven, the arena's stone foundation held it together. The wooden rows sat several hundred people. Underneath was a dungeon which held beasts of all sorts.

Lavrin was given the choice of two weapons to face his opponent. Luckily, he had been prepared by Kyra to choose wisely. He was offered a blunt mace, a long iron sword, a huge shield, a sharpened axe and a double-sided spear. He chose the sword and the spear, brandishing them with determination.

When he entered the arena, his massive opponent laughed, confident of a quick, decisive victory. The duelist cracked his knuckles and spurred the crowd to cheer his arrival.

An announcer with an echoing voice proclaimed, "To the right we have our esteemed master of the arena, who has wrestled with beasts and slain many foes. To the left we have a newcomer to our ranks, a ranger wielding sword and spear against our great champion. This man is a mystery to us all; he may be capable of greatness or fall like the rest."

As the duel began, the crowd grew silent. They were ready to watch their champion. He had a long, jagged sword and a mace. His bulky bronze armor glistened like dragon scales. Although the combatant cursed him, Lavrin remained silent and prayed for the King's aid. He wished simply to survive the day.

The man charged at Lavrin, swinging his mace violently. Lavrin had lighter armor than his opponent. This allowed him to quickly dodge the attacks. Lavrin knew he could not take this champion straight on, so he avoided him, trying to make him do something wild. When he heard the crowd laugh and gasp, the brute went into a furious rage, attacking Lavrin like a maniac. This was precisely what he wanted; he knew this would cause his opponent to either grow tired or even madder. Sliding and dodging every move, Lavrin parried each thrust that was thrown at him.

"Is this the best you've got?" Lavrin yelled. "I'm disappointed." He then ducked around his competitor, stabbing him in the back, which damaged but did not wound him. His thick armor took most of the blow. Nonetheless, his foe was weakened.

Lavrin blocked the oncoming slices, thrusts and swings with all his might, then tried to jab his spear at his rival's unprotected shoulder. He managed to catch the brute just below the collar bone. Lavrin, in return, was hit by his opponent's mace. Both stumbled back, reeling in pain. The crowd stood at attention, waiting to see who would rise first. Before either combatant could get up to continue the onslaught, Zekern ended the fight. He could not have his champion beaten by a prisoner. That might cause an uprising.

The crowd cheered for Lavrin's skill, though the battle was short. Zekern decided to reward him, even though he was his enemy. It was the custom of the arena to grant freedom to any prisoner who won a battle, but since Lavrin technically did not win, Zekern gave him two options. "You may either choose your freedom or this slave girl's." He had Kyra brought out before the crowd. Zekern knew a follower of the King would choose the girl's freedom rather than his own.

"If you give her a week's provisions, I will choose her freedom."

"Do you think that is fair?" Zekern asked the crowd.

"Yes, yes," they shouted. "Give him what he asks." They had never seen a prisoner fight so valiantly, and they wanted to see more.

"I will give her a week's food if you agree to another fight," replied Zekern, as if Lavrin had a choice in the matter. Zekern motioned for the crowd to be silent.

Softly glancing over to Kyra, Lavrin agreed. He knew he had given up the chance for his freedom, but felt the King would honor his decision. He wanted Kyra to be free and had high hopes for her and her new faith in the King. Also, Zekern would send more forces to chase after him, a strong worker and arena fighter, than after Kyra, a maiden of which he had dozens.

"Then it sounds like we have a deal." Zekern motioned to his guards.

The guards then proceeded into the arena to escort the two away, while others rushed over to the injured "champion" to offer him aid. No one tended to Lavrin's inflictions, but he fought through the agony and made his way out of the crowded arena.

******

Minutes before Kyra's departure, the two of them stood in a tower and looked through an open window of bright stained glass. The bold greens, yellows, purples and reds would have been a dazzling sight, but the two looked out over the horizon. "Head south into the forest until you reach safety," Lavrin told Kyra. "My friends can be found in the Forest of Torin. They will know what to do. If you cannot find them, continue under the cover of the trees until you reach a tree house. You should be safe there." He pointed out the direction she should head. "Do not return unless you come back with help; it is much too dangerous for you here."

With tears in her eyes, Kyra looked up at the tired but bold warrior in front of her and knew he should have freed himself. "Why did you choose me? I can't fight. You are the one who can make a difference out there. And besides, I don't know what the King wants for my life. I feel so unworthy to serve him. What can he do with someone as simple as me?"

Lavrin had wondered the same thing many times before. What could the King do with a simple ranger? The King had showed him the answer recently. Lavrin knew what to say to lift her spirits. "Although you may not know it, the King has a plan for your life, and I know that it is not for you to stay here. Besides, Zekern would desire me back more, a strong worker and the King's warrior. He would never let me leave. He would use me to find my friends and catch them, as well. But he would not expect you to find them."

After embracing Lavrin, Kyra descended the staircase with her week's food and hurried through the town. For the first time in years, someone had seen the good in her. She brushed the dust off her dress and fled into the city.

Kyra rushed through the streets of Saberlin, unsure how trustworthy Zekern's word really was. Vin also walked through the town, smelling the freshly baked bread and dodging the carts and people swarming about. Suddenly, Vin smelled something familiar. He turned and saw a young woman walking past him, almost tripping as she hurried toward the gateway.

He burst toward her, but could barely keep up. Unaware that the small terrier was following her, Kyra ducked beside a cart to hide from the guards at the gate. As

102

soon as she was far from the city, she let out a sigh of relief. She had made it this far. She took out a small piece of bread and continued toward the forest.

Kyra stepped over a long root. It was very dark in the forest, darker than she had expected, but she found her way with the rays of light which snuck through the branches.

After traveling for some time, she saw a light through the trees. Carefully, she eased toward the light which shimmered like a beacon in the darkness. Were these Lavrin's friends? She hid out of sight, crouching behind an oak tree, silently gazing at the rangers roasting meat over a fire. Vin, who had followed her all this way, bolted toward the group. Kyra froze in panic.

"Vin, how did you find us?" a man exclaimed. "I hope Lavrin is as well as you are."

Kyra, mustering all the courage she could, slowly walked into sight. "You know Lavrin?" she daringly asked.

The man stopped petting the dog. "Yes, we do. How do you know him? Do you have news of our friend?" Calix spoke urgently, hoping to gain information about Lavrin's condition.

She began to tell them what happened, and how Lavrin had earned her freedom. Grax and Calix wanted to go to Lavrin immediately, but the others promoted the idea of getting help. They were not equipped for a rescue attempt on the castle. They decided that since they would need help, it would be best to journey toward Hightenmore Castle in the Avrick Valley, northwest of Saberlin. This would allow Macrollo to deliver his letter from the King and let them find allies there. However, they still needed to get Eli and Margret to the refugee camp. They could not go back on their promise.

Although Kyra wanted to return to her family and share the good news of the King with them, she knew there would be a price on her head. Furthermore, if these rangers were planning to rescue Lavrin, she wanted to help. Though she knew nothing about these strangers, their bond to Lavrin connected her to them.

The first thing she noticed when she entered the Silent Watchers camp was that Grax was breathing hard and clutching his side. Kyra asked if she could look at his injuries. She complimented Margret on her medical skills, but noticed Grax's fever had returned. She took necessary precautions and used a better application to reduce the fever before it spread. She hoped that healing him would help her gain their trust. Grax insisted that they continue toward the refugee camp.

CHAPTER 10

THE LONG ROAD

Calix stood next to Chan as they looked across the Mud Ridge Valley. No camps were in sight, probably since they were trying to be hidden. The Mud Ridge Valley was not a regular valley; a normal valley would be smooth and grass-filled, but this was narrow and rocky, with many crevices in which to hide. So, although it was called a valley, it was truly more of a ridge. Luckily it was not deep, but it was muddy from the recent rains.

How would they find the refugee camp? Chan knew it was getting dark, but if they lit a torch, would the refugee camp respond or stay hidden? Chan went ahead with it. They would need some light. The ridge remained quiet.

As they walked along the eastern side of the valley, Nadrian suddenly tapped Chan on the shoulder. She pointed toward a crevice where she had briefly seen movement. Instead of trying to chase down the hooded person, Chan called out, "Who goes there? We mean you no harm. We have some refugees to bring to your camp."

The group lost sight of the figure until they spied three men walking toward them from a large outcropping of rock. Two held axes, but the one in the middle held no weapon. When they got closer, the group noticed their brown cloaks which served as camouflage. They wore expressions of anxiety and fear, like rabbits hiding from a fox. With suspicious eyes and arms tensed for a battle, these strangers obviously felt threatened.

After a moment, one of the three dropped his axe and rushed to Margret and Eli. He wrapped his arms around them tightly. "My son! My daughter! Glory to the marvelous King of Light. He has sent his follower a sign of his goodness. I thought I had lost you both."

Once they all were properly introduced, the three warriors lowered their guard and escorted the group up the ledges toward the middle of the ridge. Calix was thoroughly puzzled as to where they were headed. Nothing resembling a camp was recognizable.

Calix and the others were led to a stone wall, and when part of the wall was slid to the side, it opened to a huge cave. Nadrian felt her hand over the rock door as they entered, admiring the simplistic yet effective hiding place.

In the cave were about seventy people, all wearing a look of caution. As they entered, Eli's father shouted to his wife, "Look here, Lillian! These rangers have returned our children to us." Seeing the frightened gazes on the refugees' faces, he continued. "These are my honored guests!" Chan, Calix and the others were then greeted as heroes for bringing the lost children to their parents. Nadrian could tell every member of this community was treasured dearly by the rest, and everyone gingerly embraced Margret and Eli.

The cave was set up so that the weaponry was stacked near the front; the people slept and stored provisions in the back, and the tables were in the middle. The barrels and sacks were stored in a recess which had a lower temperature to help their food last longer. This room was the safest place in the cave if the valley was ever besieged. Not only was the entrance to the cave secret, but they had archer holes in which men could take cover to defend their home. They had built up this cave to be highly defensible.

"It's like an underground fortress, yet without the size or high walls," said Grax quietly as he surveyed the camp. Paintings of beautiful landscapes lined the walls in bright array. It was clear these were to give the refugees a view outside of the dark orange cavern walls.

Seated at one of the broad tables, Margret and Eli's father opened up two flasks of water. He brought out roasted turkey and carrots from the cellar. "Let us have a feast in the name of the King."

Small metal cups were passed about, and everyone got some water along with their food. To Kyra, this was the best meal she had had in months. Comparing it to prison food was the same as likening gravel to gold. The refugees had been able to salvage some tables from their houses, and the heroes were given seats next to the refugee's leader. "I see that you guide this group just as I protect my refugees," the leader said to Chan. "Do you know where you will be headed next?"

Chan looked at Macrollo. "Sadly, we have lost a close comrade to Zekern's thugs, and will need aid to get him back. Our leopard friend has told us we can find help in Hightenmore."

"I know your pain. I am now the last of my family because of those cowards. If you ever need aid in times to come, we will be ready to help you. Our weapons may be few, but our hearts are loyal and brave. You will always have a home amongst us."

The children flocked around Macrollo to feel his fur and see his sharp teeth. Kyra laughed as she saw the little ones looking at Macrollo with awe. They jumped on his back and lay their heads on his fur. He sat there, completely immovable, not wanting to harm the children. He was trapped, yet this was an imprisonment he did not desire to break out of.

Fortunately, Grax and Felloni had fully recovered from their injuries, thanks to Kyra's medical skills. She had learned a lot from her mother, who had served as a nurse many years ago. Kyra desperately wished she could talk to her mother one more time, yet her parents now lived on the eastern side of Amcronos, far out of reach.

On the other side of the room, Nadrian gave the refugee leader one of their horns so that whenever need be, they could contact each other. "This horn was given to me by Baxoni, one of the King's messengers a long time ago. I have held onto it for safe keeping. Its horn blast has been blessed by the King and can only be heard by his followers. Its sound can travel great distances in all directions. Please take this and use it to alert the King's warriors if these families you protect are ever in danger."

"May you be ever blessed for your charity," replied the leader.

Chan was given a letter by the refugees' leader to deliver to the Lord of Hightenmore. It appeared they were not the only ones wishing for aid from Hightenmore's gates. Chan carefully placed it in the safety of an inner pocket, making sure it was completely tucked away.

It was decided by Margret and Eli's father that the horses should go on to Hightenmore with the group. The cave was not large enough to house them, and they would likely be noticed by outsiders if they remained in the valley. Furthermore, Calix and the others had a far greater need for them. Chan agreed to bring them back at a later time, when they received word of the family's safe return home.

After a night's sleep, the journey to Hightenmore began with the seven of them setting off into the Forest of Bane. Calix knew this forest like the back of his hand, so they passed the trees and thick overgrown grass with determination and speed. They found some food along the way, such as berries and nuts, but mostly ate from their rations.

As they traveled, they spoke about everything that had occurred at the camp. Chan chuckled heartily as Nadrian retold the misery Macrollo had endured for the children's sake. "If any part of my fur has been ripped out, please tell me," Macrollo said. "I truly hope they did not damage my coat."

"Didn't you always have that empty spot on your back?" Grax remarked.

Frantically, Macrollo tried to investigate, before everyone else began to laugh. "He was only joking. You are fine," Calix said.

"I don't know about all of you, but I'm just glad we were able to eat a warm meal and meet more followers of the King. I am so blessed to be free of my prison cell." Kyra twirled her hair as she walked.

"I have felt that way before, but never like I've felt it recently," Nadrian said. "What do you think, Felloni?"

A puzzled gaze spread across his face. "I'm glad you all enjoyed it."

Grax's brow furrowed. "Did you not appreciate your time in the cavern, Felloni? The rest of us surely did."

Felloni grimaced. "I am still thinking of our losses. A fact you have too easily forgotten."

Everyone's thoughts returned to the fateful hour. Everyone except for Kyra and Macrollo, who kept their spirits up, and eagerly awaited the majesty of Hightenmore castle.

The trek through the forest took them two days, and by the time they were through, they were very tired. Despondently, they had little provisions left for the seven of them. Vin panted often, but was still the most energetic, as most dogs are. He had waited a long time outside of the camp, and was glad to now be back with the group.

******

Although the sun beat down on the seven, it was nothing compared to Lavrin's pain. Thrashes stung his back, and his hands ached from pulling loads of bricks. Lavrin had been working all day and night with only one meal. The slave masters displayed angry scowls which seemed to strike at the very souls of their captives.

"At least I do not have to battle in the arena for the rest of the week," Lavrin said to himself. This glimmer of positive thinking was the only way he kept going. Along with many other slaves, Lavrin was forced to make and haul loads of bricks for Zekern's next project: a new barracks for his expanding army. It slowly grew in size, and began to take form as a building. The hours crawled by at a dreadful pace. The slaves seemed to have abandoned the possibility of hope. They were becoming more like work animals than humans, focused only on dragging large quantities of heavy red bricks.

Many worked so hard that they passed out or died, but Lavrin knew of the King's plan for him. The overseers did not care if men fainted; they only placed them to the side, and made the rest of the force work harder. Lavrin knew that if he did die, he would be free from his bondage and live with his Lord in the Haven Realm, the place where everything was perfect.

Lavrin flashed back to the second arena battle he had recently fought. He recalled sitting in his empty, forlorn, desolate lockup...waiting. Eventually, the rats scurried away in fright as the jail warden approached Lavrin's confinement. The time had arrived.

The cold-hearted warden shifted the keys in his hand, and found the slender one which unlocked Lavrin's cell. Lavrin willingly followed him to the miniscule room leading to the arena. He could already hear the chanting thunder of the droves of entertainment-hungry citizens in the arena's stands.

Determinedly, Lavrin gazed at the rack of weapons. Since he had asked around, he knew a decent amount about his opponent. Apparently, his adversary was fast and headstrong, preferring a straight forward approach. Many claimed he had no defensive capabilities but was fully focused on the offensive, trying to overwhelm his foe.

Thus, Lavrin decided to arm himself with a strong iron shield and a long one-handed sword. He imagined that if he could cease his opponent's offensive onslaught for even a second, he could strike him when vulnerable.

112

Hearing the announcer call forth his name, Lavrin tightened his gloves. Striding out onto the battlefield, Lavrin was greeted with both loud cheers and angry rejections. He paid no attention to the people Zekern had so effectively corrupted.

His foe carried twin blades with skulls on their hilts. This unruly, wild looking man snarled viciously at Lavrin. Lavrin began to view him as a panther or bear, not a human being. In fact, his opponent was so rugged and extreme, he slid his blade across his hand, just to reveal his tolerance to pain. Lavrin cringed.

As Lavrin expected, the wild man started the fight, flinging himself freakishly at Lavrin. He was so bent on chaos that he ran toward Lavrin like a hyena. Lavrin was fully prepared and slammed his shield headfirst toward the charging man, knocking him back.

Once more he attacked, and Lavrin calmly locked his blade with one of his pursuers and thrust it aside. On several occasions the man's furious yet skillful strikes almost damaged Lavrin, but he remained true to his plan.

Though Lavrin had risked getting stabbed, his defensive strategy paid off and the other duelist tired. From there it was a simple matter of unhinging the man's sword and kicking him in his chest.

After the man fell, Lavrin placed the tip of his blade on his opponent's neck, then simply walked back toward the prison. Though the crowd was thoroughly upset, Lavrin witnessed a look of gratitude from the unkempt man that he

113

would never forget. It was honest and sincere, coming from his very heart. "Maybe there is more to that man than I thought," Lavrin whispered to himself quietly.

Lavrin awoke from his flashback just in time, before the overseers struck him in the back. He continued his work, eagerly awaiting its end. A few hours later, when Lavrin was mopping the dungeon, a rotting aroma filling the humid air, a litz brought him a message. A litz is a small, sparrow-sized dragon that can fly faster than most common birds. Although they are often hunted for the rare gem on their back, they are excellent messengers. This litz was dark green with a ruby red gem.

Fortunately, Lavrin was alone when the litz flew in, because if he had not been, he never would have been able to read this message:

My friend,

Do not lose hope in the King. He is always ready to aid a follower in need. Your companions are safe and continuing their quest. You are doing the right thing by not rejecting Him as they hassle you to do. We will be coming for you soon, Lavrin, but stay strong, for the King has not yet said that the time is right. Your act of kindness to the maiden was not unnoticed by the King. The great King of Light, may he live and reign forever, and may his followers prosper!

A Ranger of the King

Few could have endured what Lavrin endured, but the King was with him. This brought comfort to his sorrow and peace to his never-ending pain.

******

Chan decided to pass through the rough town of Ken Van to find some supplies. Gangs were common in this town, as there was no real order in place. Smaller gangs commonly rebelled against the leading gang. Wine flowed freely as people tried to fill the emptiness inside them. Not surprisingly, this caused many people of the town to act very foolishly.

Most civilians traveled on foot across the dirt roads, but occasionally horses trotted by. Screaming and yelling could be heard as Chan and the others entered. Two small mobs were squaring off - one armed with clubs, the other with whips.

Hostility shown in their eyes. They cast dark looks toward each other and readied their brutish weapons to strike. The men did not care about the lives their needless actions would affect. They did not care about the families torn apart or the lives ended, as long as they got their moment of power.

The innocent bystanders hid their faces. They made sure to walk as far away from the skirmish as possible, afraid to be dragged into the affair. They had seen many encounters like this before; they knew they never ended well.

Chan guided the team away from the brawl as well, to make sure they were not forced to fight. They wanted to pick up supplies and head off toward Hightenmore. The longer they waited, the higher the chances that they would be caught up in something.

Nadrian stared in sadness at the brutal people of this town. "Is there no peace here?"

Looking across the scene, the group was not impressed by what they discovered. There was little culture, history or respect that could be found anywhere in the town. It had not always been this way, but over time deceit and the plague of pride had crept in. People began to be more stubborn and hateful, only caring for themselves. This led to its slow downfall. It had potential as a city, but was weighed down by deceit and despair.

As they entered the market, the team was dismayed by the high prices and stubborn merchants, unwilling to lower their prices a penny. Many poor peasants were left trying to survive on street corners. "A king would barely be able to buy these goods," Grax said jokingly. The group

116

knew they would have to continue on without buying supplies here. They would have to reach Hightenmore with what they had left.

"I wish we could help these people," Kyra remarked. "When we have freed Lavrin, we need to make sure Hightenmore does something about this. The poor citizens of Ken Van should not have to suffer this way."

When they turned a corner, they overheard two men talking. "I hear there is a reward on that slave girl who escaped Saberlin."

"I would love to get my hands on that gold. What would you do with it if you caught her?" the other man said.

He snickered to himself. "Tough to say. Moving out of this filthy town would be my first thought. Then maybe buy a fancy house somewhere in Saberlin."

The group quickly hurried away. Kyra bit her lip, fighting back a flood of panic. The pity she had felt for these people now turned to terror. She did not want to return to Saberlin as a prisoner. The rest of the group comforted her, but she still felt the weight of the moment on her shoulders.

As the team was about to leave the town, a man in a small hut called to them. It was so small it could barely be called a house, but it appeared in decent repair. Unlike its vulgar surroundings, there was a quaint feeling about this little yellow home. The middle-aged man looked past them, then motioned toward them. "Come in here. My name is Matthais, and I help all followers of the King."

Hesitantly, they entered and gazed upon a large painting of a great battle. Knights lined the horizon carrying spears and lances. At the forefront of the painting, two knights locked swords and stood their ground against the other. It was a masterful work and an utterly breathtaking scene, yet the man made sure to note that he had not painted it.

Kyra glanced back to make sure the two men were not following them. She felt more and more afraid of Ken Van and wanted to flee as far as she possibly could from it. Though she would never last long on her own, she suddenly wished she was, at least for the others' safety.

The man brushed his thin head of hair as he brought out a purple and golden book and opened it with a key. He handed it to them, and they flipped through its pages in awe. The book contained stories of knights and maidens, disasters and floods, and was the greatest record of the King's followers they had ever seen. Its calligraphy was flawless, and its strokes were masterful. The man revealed that he secretly had been making copies of the King's book and distributing them to his followers. It was a passion of his, and he was glad to report that the copies were still being spread about. Yet making these brilliant works took time, so he had only managed to compile a few of them.

"Great are the things destined for you all; you will serve the King very well, indeed," the man stated. "That book is for you. Cherish it and the stories it holds." Felloni stored it safely away under his cloak. He knew that this book was of great importance. It would be one of the mightiest tools to use for the King as a testimony to his wise ways and his faithful followers.

"How did you know we follow the King?" Felloni asked.

"I didn't at first, but when I spotted Macrollo, whom I know well, I knew you were of the King's faithful. Now, you must not linger here. It is not safe; you must leave at once." He continued to Kyra, "There is a bounty on your head, young lady. You must be careful. Come to me for counsel or anything you need in the future."

"Do you think Hightenmore will accept us?" Grax questioned.

Matthais grinned. "Hightenmore will treat you very kindly, especially with Macrollo at your side. I honestly wish I could live there myself, but I am needed here to help this despondent place however I can."

"You could travel with us if you desired. We plan to leave for Hightenmore immediately," Calix said.

Matthais' grin turned to a frown. "Like I said, I am needed here. Hopefully, your mission turns out to be a complete success. I only wish the best for all of you. May the brightest star of the sky and the guiding hand of the King lead your footsteps."

Everyone thanked him for his kindness, and Macrollo thanked Matthais for once again being there for him. Matthais whispered to Macrollo, "Make sure you protect them, they need to reach Hightenmore safely."

The team then departed the scribe's hut and proceeded out of town quickly. With a sense of urgency, yet relief, the team traveled north toward Hightenmore. Hope swelled within them as they neared ever closer to the mighty citadel.

A long road lay before them and possibly one of the most important battles of their lives. The opposition would be great, and although they were empowered by the King and encouraged through their hope, evil would be waiting at their doorstep. The question still loomed in their minds - what trials awaited them on the road to Hightenmore?

CHAPTER 11

LOYALTY

Over the next couple of days they made excellent headway - half way to Hightenmore from Ken Van. The group effortlessly found their way through the brush. Although this forest was new to them, its paths were far easier to find. The trees themselves seemed to step aside, allowing them passage.

They were focused on reaching Hightenmore. Everything would be all right if they could reach Hightenmore. Of course it would…it had to be.

It seemed like a wonderful place. Calix had heard rumors in Saberlin of Hightenmore's security and prosperity. People called it the Sanctuary of Men and the

Place of Peace. Calix could only hope these references were true.

Still, he realized trying to break Lavrin out of Saberlin's dungeons could be seen as act of hostility. If Hightenmore really was a place of peace, it may not want a fight with Saberlin. This would ruin their chance of saving Lavrin. There was still hope, however, because the soldiers of Hightenmore were acclaimed throughout the Northwest as valiant warriors.

Eventually, Calix let his worries fade. As he shifted the weight of his pack, he was relieved to hear Grax say, "This seems like a suitable place to set up for the night. We will need plenty of rest before continuing toward Hightenmore in the morning."

Chan laid his pack on the ground. "We will need someone to stand watch during the night, just in case. Everyone will get time to recover when we reach our destination. Do we have any volunteers?"

"I will," Macrollo said. "I owe you all a favor for helping me with those nasty fire hounds. I'm fortunate you came to my aid when you did - those beasts could have done horrible things to me."

Vin and Macrollo were used to staying up late, so they hunted while the others slept. They caught a deer, and though this was a fine catch, they had hoped to find a fresh water source nearby. They dragged the deer back to camp with little effort. Later in the night, Macrollo tended the fire alone, roasting the meat as Vin drifted into sleep. The fire slowly dwindled as a dense fog rolled in, and the ivory moon was hidden in the sky. A serene feeling washed over Macrollo as he watched his friends rest in the light of the flickering fire. He stoked the fire back to life as it swayed this way and that.

Macrollo stood up and stretched. He was tired from the journey, yet he needed to keep their fire going. Who knew what could be roaming about these woods?

As he stepped away for a moment to gather more firewood, Macrollo noticed a large grouping of sticks near a broad tree. He bent down and picked up as many as he could with his paws. While trying to gather the firewood, he was smashed to the ground by a huge black boar. Twigs flew everywhere as Macrollo slammed onto the firm forest floor. He freed himself from the boar's grip and bashed it into a tree. The boar staggered up, red eyes glaring. It charged at Macrollo, but he pounced on top of it and embedded his claw in its side. It struggled to be free from his grip, but Macrollo forced it downward. Its eyes clearly reflected its state of shock.

Just as the boar died, the band of hunters who had been chasing it eyed Macrollo. They had been roaming the woods south of Hightenmore, hoping to catch any creatures they could. They knew Macrollo's fur would be worth much, and seeing the King's emblem on his vest, knew Zekern would be pleased with his death. Truthfully, they were not loyal to Zekern, but only wanted what would earn them a handsome sum. Gaining favor with Zekern could profit them greatly.

The hunters wore ragged cloaks, and although they had excellent aim, they had no armor that could endure a sword, arrow, or any weapon for that matter. Skins hung over their shoulders from an earlier catch. They looked toward Macrollo with sharp, glaring intent. He could tell they wanted him dead. A creature of such majesty would bring enough riches for all of them.

The five hunters skillfully surrounded him by lurking in the shadows of the trees and launching arrows from behind their branches. Macrollo climbed a tree and pounced downward, sending one hurling. When he leapt toward the next tree, an arrow met his shoulder, and he fell. The wound was deep, but Macrollo knew he could recover from it. He must recover.

Quickly, the hunters aided their teammate, while Macrollo struggled to get a footing. Although he wanted to escape from the current threat, the shock from the gnawing pain stunned him. Eventually rising, Macrollo angrily growled at the swift, bold hunters who turned toward him. Embracing his true leopard prowess, Macrollo went on all fours and swept his tail about menacingly. With looks of uncertainty, the hunters peered at his drawn claws and aimed their bows to fire.

Macrollo dove behind a tree, barely dodging their shots. His shoulder stung, so he ripped out the arrow. Macrollo dared to move to a position closer to them. They noticed and backed away. Macrollo knew he needed help; these hunters were seasoned in taking out animals.

Meanwhile, the hunters whispered to one another, "Why doesn't he come out?"

Suddenly, Macrollo reached a claw around the tree. One of the hunters instinctively fired at his paw. He pulled it back when he heard the bow fire.

Seeing this act of cleverness, the hunters turned toward one another. Their gazes locked. "He can think. What are we fighting against here?"

"I am as human as you are," Macrollo called out to them. "Leave me alone and let me return to my friends."

"There are more of his kind?" One of the hunters turned to his fellow tracker. "We should capture him and take him in for the highest bidder."

Though they did not realize it, Macrollo overheard their conversation. It was too much for him. He thought of his comrades so close to Hightenmore. They would chase his hunters back toward Saberlin if he was caught. If his friends followed them back to Saberlin, they would die. He could not allow it.

Macrollo pounced from his hiding place and charged at the men. They missed him with their initial attacks, and he knocked one of them out of the way with a heavy thrust.

Believing their lives were in danger, the remaining three fired rapidly. Two of the three shafts struck into Macrollo's chest, and the final tore into his leg. He tried to cry out in pain, but only a small whimper escaped. The onslaught of inflictions was too much for him to overcome.

Seeing that they had defeated him, the cautious hunters slowly crept toward the leopard's body and felt his smooth fur. The five of them managed to carry his weight together. One of them looked at Macrollo with a heavy heart, wondering if they had killed an innocent being. They had slayed many beasts before, but Macrollo was different.

When the hunters began to walk away, Grax came charging in, axes swinging furiously. He let loose a mighty war cry. Dropping the leopard, they fled, afraid that others may be on their way.

Macrollo lost consciousness as his heart slowly slipped from the world. Picking up his fallen friend, Grax somberly left the bloody scene. Grax carried Macrollo's body to the camp and, now awake, the others were shocked and confused to see Grax's heavy tears. He moaned loudly, like he had lost a family member.

Everyone was instantly torn from the inside out. They had not gotten to know Macrollo long, but everything that they had learned about him now grieved them. He was a great follower of the King and had the heart of a diamond, pure and valuable. Kyra shielded her eyes in grief, and Nadrian rose and paced about to and fro. Calix helped Grax lay down their friend. They remembered how brave and how loyal of a companion Macrollo had been. Little did they know that his last act had been to save them. They could not hold back tears.

After Macrollo had been buried, they took the arrows, stabbed them in the ground, and set rocks around them as a marker of the tragedy. Many may pass and think nothing of the memorial, but it would always hold a place in their hearts.

Though they knew Macrollo's death was not their fault, they still blamed themselves. Grax was the worst of all, torn by the grief that he could have rushed to save Macrollo sooner, or taken the night shift in his stead.

Grax relayed the tragic event to the others, forcing each word out. Chan held the letter which Macrollo fought to defend. He knew Hightenmore Castle was close, yet the team was tired. There was probably a search party looking for them at that very moment. The bounty on Kyra still remained. In the back of his mind, Chan wondered if they had been followed from Ken Van. Against their wishes, he made the team move on. The pitter patter of rain and the sound of branches rustling in the wind were ever-present reminders that the mission was not over. Their boots slopped in the mud, and the fog clouded their vision. Chan knew the team's comfort was not worth slowing down their task, but nonetheless he longed to comfort them.

Chan knew the message was important, yet he did not know the true importance of the smooth parchment he placed in his belt pouch. Even though they could hear horses and footsteps in the distance, they traveled slowly.

Felloni gave Kyra a dagger for self-defense, realizing any one of them could be in danger now. She held it awkwardly before placing it in the sheath he gave her. He wanted to make sure they did not lose anyone else. Calix also sensed the danger and thus felt a deep urgency to get to Hightenmore. Lavrin was taken and, no doubt, enduring much pain. Macrollo was dead. Hightenmore was his chance to help Lavrin and honor Macrollo's sacrifice.

As they crossed the Avrick Valley, they saw the grand castle like a royal jewel on a golden crown. Hightenmore towered in front of them, a mighty fortress with broad stone walls and elevated towers. It was home to followers of the King. Most of all, it was a source of great hope.

Passing the farmers' homes and fields scattered across the valley, the group eventually stood on a broad dirt road entering Hightenmore. A pair of guards stood at attention in front of the gate. The guards wore the Hightenmore emblem with pride. After Calix explained their desire to enter, the two looked at each other. They had not expected this arrival, but knew the lord would be pleased with a message from the King. The guards escorted them into the Great Hall and to the table where Lord Auden, head of the castle, was seated.

The hall was spacious, and although it was ornate, it was open for all followers of the King to dine and discuss important matters. A golden chandelier hung from the ceiling, and embroidered tablecloths adorned each of the oak tables. Both rich and poor sat at these tables, and even peasants were not treated as outcasts. There was a deep bond between the townspeople that could not be broken.

Although the group greatly enjoyed the rich, steaming food offered to them, their sorrow was nonetheless obvious. Everyone wished Macrollo was there eating with them. They longed to talk to him one last time. "Why are you downcast?" the lord asked, seeing their grieving faces.

"We do not mean to distress you, Lord Auden," Calix replied. "We have lost one friend to bandits and another was killed by hunters. We wish they could have enjoyed this time with us, especially since it was our slain friend's mission which brought us to you in the first place. We have come because he was delivering you a message from the King."

"I am sorry for your loss, but I have good news for you. My spies have informed me that your other friend is alive, although he is still under Zekern's harsh reign. He has been forced to battle in Zekern's arena several times now. We can only hope that he will continue to win these duels, because Zekern will continue to have him fight. The King has seen your plight. He instructed me to send ten of our top spies to try to save your friend. It may, however, take time to get them fully prepared for such a difficult task. Zekern has many guards circling the city. He has many more soldiers than his father ever considered having."

After the feast, Chan gave Auden the letter. It relieved him to have finally delivered it to its destination. He also showed Lord Auden the message from the refugee camp. Auden kindly thanked Chan for his resolve in getting the letters to him, and assured him the refugee camp would be treated well.

129

After the group got some rest, they walked down to the burial grounds, west of the main castle, yet still inside the inner wall. Auden had allowed them to set up a burial marker in remembrance of Macrollo. They dressed in black to honor their friend's sacrifice. "Macrollo, great leopard warrior and servant of the King, thank you for protecting us and giving us your companionship," they said as the marker was placed. "Your mission is complete; rest now in the King's peace."

Back in the Great Hall, Lord Auden anxiously sat down and opened the precious note from the King of Light. He savored its crisp paper, like it was pure gold. Anything from the King deserved such respect. Auden could hardly withhold his intrigue and enthusiasm to hear what the King had planned for him in the near future. Yet what he read was not a joyous note, it was a serious warning. This was what the message stated:

Dear Auden,

You have trained your warriors well and have always remembered to follow my ways. Prepare yourself. Zekern's forces will march toward you soon and he will be brutal against you. Do not fear, for I will aid you. Remember the lighthouse you built and make sure to have catapults placed on the inner wall. Be sure to have the scouts you are sending to help Lavrin wait until Saberlin is emptied.

The King of Light

"This is distressing news, but I knew this time would come sooner or later." Auden said to Chan, who had entered the Great Hall a few moments prior.

He read over the letter. "How does the King know of Zekern's impending attack?"

"The King works in strange ways. Many have said that he can tell of events before they come to pass," Lord Auden replied. "Although this attack seems horrible now, it may help with Lavrin's escape. In the meantime, I need to prepare my city."

The soldiers at Hightenmore quickly assembled the catapults using precisely cut stone and wood. The five catapults, which took great effort to make, were placed on strategic spots on the inner wall.

The lighthouse was on the eastern side, in view of the harbor and the sea, and was a beacon of hope to the soldiers of the castle. Grax helped the blacksmith make new weapons for the troops, and Hightenmore was busy with preparations and planning.

The civilians began to store food inside Hightenmore's tunnel system, and farmers gathered their crops in case they needed to evacuate their homes. The people had not feared a major attack on Hightenmore's strong walls for quite some time. They were used to peaceful times under the King. They were shocked at

Zekern's nerve to plan such a feat, but were assured that the King would help them withstand the assault. The great castle of Hightenmore would not fall without a fight.

CHAPTER 12

PREPARATIONS

Hightenmore had three layers of defense: an outer wall, an inner wall and the castle. The outer wall had three points of entry guarded by giant free-standing crossbows and thick wooden gates. About three-fourths of the guards were stationed there. Between the outer and inner walls, the knights resided in modest homes.

Beyond the outer walls of the castle in the Avrick Valley, the peasants dwelt in straw and wood huts and tended to their farms. Bell towers were scattered throughout the villages to sound for help whenever necessary. Some knights were stationed in the villages to maintain peace and justice, and to make sure the people were loyal. Lord Auden was very merciful to his people compared to the rulers of neighboring cities, and only received a small income through taxes, which he used wisely.

The inner wall of Hightenmore was thicker, but made of stone as well. New catapults rested atop it. The inner wall surrounded the castle and was the main defense against naval attacks.

Between the inner wall and the castle, Hightenmore's blacksmith labored in his shop with his apprentices. The smiths of this castle were said to rival those throughout Amcronos.

The burial grounds were located on the southwest part of the estate within the inner wall. There was also a small, well-kept stable which held fine horses, about fifteen to twenty in number.

The castle was where the lord and his family resided. His personal guard attended him at all times. The castle was strong, and had a large storage room for supplies and weapons in a time of need. The castle's well had a secret entry to the tunnels underground. There was also a tunnel entry in the inner and outer walls. The tunnels were the location of the dungeons and were the fastest way to get throughout the castle.

Hightenmore had about five hundred soldiers, not including peasants, women and children. These soldiers were highly trained, practicing swordsmanship and battle formations for many hours each day. Knowing they were protected by these loyal knights, refuges and followers of the King came to Hightenmore and the Avrick Valley every year. It was the main place where followers of the King could live in peace.

Some peasants joined the army for pay, but many joined because they loved the King and felt a duty to fight. Most of the soldiers were archers or footmen, and each was required to have at least one month of training in bow, sword or whatever weapon they chose. After they had trained, they were fitted for armor before being knighted by the Lord.

Chan, Calix, Nadrian, Kyra, Grax and Felloni were brought to the gardens where Auden sat on a stone bench. Auden invited them to sit across from him. "I know you have been through many challenges lately, and are probably wondering where to go next. You must have faced many adversities to get here, both physical and emotional."

He stood and began to pace. "I need strong, able soldiers like you to defend against the coming threat. Truthfully, people who are as passionate for the King as you would make great additions to my army. Even though we've barely met, I know you would be, and in many ways already are, excellent knights. It will mean you will not live in the forest as much, but you might not miss the forest life as much as it may seem. Would you like to be knighted for the King under the Hightenmore banner?"

Calix looked at the others, then stood. "All my life I have lived in the forest, loving the King but never truly standing out for him. Lord Auden, I will join your army. Lavrin and I have longed for this chance for years. Maybe being a knight will make me twice the soldier I ever was."

Felloni arose soon after. "Although it will be hard, I will join your army as well. Perhaps there will be knowledge and adventure to be gained along the way."

A few moments of silence passed. "What about the rest of you?" Auden asked. "You do not need to do this. Only do what you feel is your calling."

"My axe is yours to use for the King," Grax replied.

Nadrian and Chan gazed at each other. They had never left their team before; for that matter, neither had they ever left their free-roaming ways. They knew either way they could still serve the King.

Simultaneously they stood and answered, "We would be honored to join, and even die, for you in service of the King."

Kyra took her time to answer. "I do not believe I have the strength to be a knight, but I would wish to help in other ways. I know a lot about healing. Are you in need of any doctors?"

"You are very humble," Auden said. "Yes, we do, in fact, need well-trained doctors. I'm sure you will save many lives here." He turned to all of them. "Thank you for your willingness; please come tonight to the throne room so you can receive the honor you deserve. Although you will still need training, this will be a sign that you have been worthy knights from the beginning."

While Auden escorted the group back to the hall, blacksmiths forged new weapons for the guards. Meanwhile, masons gauged the gaps in the walls and filled them, preparing for the rising threat.

******

Later that day, in Hightenmore's hall, the six of them gathered and sat near Auden. He had just finished settling a dispute between two townsmen, who had asked whether or not to slaughter the farm's animals before the invasion. He had wisely dealt with their concerns and turned to his new soldiers.

Lord Auden had five swords, each crafted of pure metal with a handle woven of fine leather. First, Felloni knelt before him. "Felloni, brother and friend, skilled warrior and silent ranger. I knight you in the King's name." He handed Felloni a sword with a leopard on the hilt. Auden also granted him a wonderful horn made of ivory and engraved with silver. "Use this to call us in times of need." Felloni bowed and stepped aside, admiring the sword's craftsmanship.

Nadrian then knelt at Auden's side. Auden carefully considered each word before speaking. "Nadrian, maiden of the mist, long has the King waited for you to follow his path," Auden proclaimed. "You are now becoming all you were meant to be. You are a skilled bowman and huntress, impatient yet fearless as you use your talents for the King's cause. I am glad to have you at my side." Auden presented a sword with a wolf on its hilt and also gave her a silken arrow with a silver tip. "It is my best arrow; use it wisely."

Chan stepped forward. "Rise, Chan, leader of rangers. You have done well in your struggle to overcome Zekern's forces. Your judgment is sound. Although you have traveled a weary road, you have clung to your ever-growing faith in the King. You have roused your teammates together throughout this campaign. You are a great fighter and loyal friend. For the leadership you have shown, I will make you a commander." Auden gave him a sword with the emblem of a hawk. He also gave him a map of all Amcronos. "To never lose your way," Auden said.

Grax was next to kneel before Lord Auden, who placed his hand on Grax's shoulder. "Tall warrior of the forest, your axe will continue to smite many a foe in your path. The King has blessed you with a strong body and a wise heart. Your way is pure and loyal. Never was there a better warrior to have at one's side. May the King guard and keep you." Auden granted him a sword with a bear and the gift of dark leather gloves.

To Calix, Auden nodded with eyes of compassion. "You have lost many an ally on this quest, but do not feel down-hearted; your righteous fury and persistence are unmatched in the land. Your battle techniques are flawless, and your motives pure. You are faithful in the big and small things, and for this the King will be faithful to you forever, as he has promised. I know you will follow the King the rest of your days." Calix was handed a sword with a rearing stallion as its crest. He was also given a dark blue litz with

138

an orange gem on its back. "Funny creatures, those litz are; they are great messengers and fine friends," Auden remarked.

"And to you, Kyra. I hope you can find your place in this world," Auden continued. "I give you this jar of rare healing spices, together with this book of medicine. May your healing be blessed and save many lives. In addition, here is a special bracelet, crafted by our finest smiths." It was an ornate piece, and Kyra especially liked the deer engraved upon it.

Facing the group of six, Auden smiled as if a proud father. "Tonight there is a meeting with my advisors, to which I would like to invite you. We have a crucial decision to make regarding the oncoming attack from Zekern's forces. Welcome to my ranks, honorable rangers of the woods."

******

Lord Auden, Calix, Kyra, Chan, Grax, Nadrian, Felloni and Auden's five top advisors gathered around the central table in the hall. A map lay upon it, Hightenmore on one end and Saberlin at the other.

Auden started the meeting by addressing his advisors. "Through these six, we have recovered a message from the King, which has informed us of a potential threat: Saberlin is mounting an army with which they plan to assault Hightenmore. We have known ever since Zekern's father died that things have changed in Saberlin. We never quite guessed that the threat would come so soon. Our guards have recently discovered a spy from Saberlin who is now in the dungeons. They pressed him for information, but he would not say anything about Zekern's plans or whereabouts. What is our best course of action? Do we need help from the nearby cities?"

"The letter gives no information about this army Zekern is forming, besides that it was a threat?" one of the nobles asked.

"That is correct."

Another noble with red hair and a small goatee spoke up. "The guards only managed to find one of Zekern's scouts? That's disappointing. If only we had better means by which to make him speak."

The first noble disagreed. "We have never used extreme methods unless absolutely necessary."

"Maybe they are necessary!" the other replied harshly.

Whispers broke out across the table until they turned into arguing, then snapping, until Auden finally stood up and silenced them, slamming his fist onto the table. "Don't you see this is what Zekern wants? Confusion, bickering and disunity - if we cannot find a solution, all will be lost. Not while I still have the King's blood in my veins will I let such rubbish cripple the castle of Hightenmore!" He sat down decisively.

"You're right, Lord Auden," Nadrian said. "There must be some plan we can agree upon."

"So, what do you suggest?" Auden asked.

She thought for a moment. "I think we need more information. Not only do we need to know their plans, but also how close they are to having their army ready. The easiest way would be to pressure the prisoner until he speaks, but that is not the most honorable way. If we send scouts into Saberlin to bring back information, we will be sure of the facts. We could never tell if the prisoner was speaking the truth. "

"True, but how long do you think it will take to get this information?" one advisor asked.

"About a week to a week and a half, for both the journey there and the return," the general, fifth advisor to Auden, said. "We should have enough time to make preparations if they aren't already heading our way. We'll need to hire more guards and arm them. This siege could be devastating if we are not ready for it."

Auden bit his lip as he considered this alarming possibility, but then quickly calmed himself. "That sounds fine. But when can we have these spies sent out, General?"

"My troops are always prepared. We can have them ready by sunrise. I will send my top scouts. I'm sure they will not fail us."

Auden could have guessed that was what his general would have said. "Good. Make sure they are disguised to look like townsfolk, so Zekern's guards will not be suspicious."

"It will be done, my lord," the general replied. Quietly, they left the hall. The general readied his twelve fastest men and made sure they knew the importance of their mission.

As the general had so confidently assured, his men were ready. They hid their weapons in their farmers' clothing. They rushed out of Hightenmore with purpose. They had been trained for moments like this, there was no time for uncertainty.

Workers from across the city were called into action as the castle prepared for battle. It was a very long, laborious process. Everyone pitched in, even the elderly. Lord Auden drafted more men as guards, and their training began immediately.

CHAPTER 13

SURVIVAL

The early morning breeze blew steadily across the land. It was sunrise, and the sky glowed purple, orange and pink. Twelve men, dressed in rags and appearing unarmed, traveled quickly through the valley and into the forest. It seemed as if their whole lives were meant for this day.

They were determined; no force would stop them. They knew their mission and what was expected of them. Yet as the day progressed, it seemed as though they were going too fast. It was too easy. They were three hours ahead of schedule, so they set up camp for the night. They rested their bodies and hearts, knowing their mission was dangerous. Each went over his assignment in his head as they sat around the fire.

After seven hours of sleep, they awoke, packed up and headed through the forest where they found a river. They followed the flowing river for the length of the day until they figured they were two-thirds of the way through the forest. They stopped at the river's end, unpacked some of their provisions and made a small fire with what little they could find. Soon after, they found their way to a deep, peaceful sleep.

The next day, they finally left the forest and entered a small town near the outskirts of Saberlin. They bought two carts filled with enough wheat and pitchforks for half of them. As they wheeled the carts toward Saberlin, it started to rain. The men knew the rain would not help things - now they would have to wait until morning to begin searching for information.

Reaching the high metal gates of Saberlin, one of the twelve said to the guards, "Please let us enter. We are wet and need to store this wheat."

"Why didn't you have your horses wheel the carts here instead of lugging them yourselves?" a guard replied.

"We are poor and our one horse has been taken from us. Our crops have not prospered the last few years, and this year we hope for a better outcome. Please pity us, sir. This grain may feed your family in the future."

The guards circled the wagons and then opened the gates. With looks of scorn, the soldiers of Saberlin pointed toward the city. "You may enter."

Soon they were out of the rain. The spies wheeled the carts into an alleyway and helped the others crawl out. Although they were not in need of much money, they decided to sell the wheat to not arouse suspicion. Next, they found an inn where they could steer clear of curious eyes. People were everywhere, and they did not know who they could trust.

Upon waking the next morning, they divided into six groups. Each group went to a strategic location to learn what they could about Zekern's army: the tavern, the street, the stores, the noble's estates, the market and the arena where many had gathered for the gladiator show. Each position had a route for easy escape. Luckily the rain had stopped, and each group experienced little difficulty reaching their location.

At the tavern, people slowly gathered for their rounds of ale and daily talk. Two of the scouts sat at a small corner table. While waiting to be served, they anxiously peered from side to side across the room. When the server arrived and asked what they wanted, they simply replied, "Water, please."

The suspicious woman looked at them queerly, and then brought out two cups of water. "Will that be all for you strangers?"

"Yes. Say, do you know who to talk to about the gladiator fights? They seem like quite the occasion around here." He tried to sound as normal as possible.

"You must be new. There are few newcomers entering Saberlin as of late. Anyway, see that man over there? He may know what you're looking for."

They thanked her with a small tip and walked over to his table. The perplexed man sat there whispering to someone they assumed was his friend. "I hope I'm not disturbing you, sir, but may we have a word?" the scout asked, hoping not to lose his favor.

"I suppose." The man hiccupped, obviously full of wine.

One of the scouts was going to sit down, but the other pulled him aside. "It's not wise to question someone who is drunk. I'm sure there's someone else here who can help us."

"How do we know if there's anyone here who's not drunk? We are in a tavern."

"Don't give up hope yet."

The two soon found their luck as they began talking with an elderly lady mending clothes in the corner of the room. She was frail and poor, but still knew a lot about the happenings of the town. Most importantly, she was open to talking with them. The clothes she was fixing looked in desperate shape, yet she was undeterred by the task. The two spies realized this hard job might be her only means to provide for herself. They pitied her and wished they could help.

They wondered if anyone who was not a servant of Zekern could have a decent life here. Was everyone in the city struggling to get by just because of one wicked ruler?

The lady continued her work. "What are you young fellows doing in this part of town? Please, I pray you're not tax collectors."

"No, ma'am, we are not. Why? Is something wrong?"

She sighed. "With Zekern's new taxes, it is impossible for a widow like me to make a good living. It's especially hard when fewer and fewer people need me to mend their clothes."

"What kind of taxes? Maybe we can help."

She was shocked. "Oh my dear boys, you do not need to help an old lady with her affairs, but thank you for your kindness. The taxes have been around since Zekern became lord. For the last year, Zekern has been growing his army. A large group of troops arrived yesterday. He parades his men on occasion to keep us scared. He must have around nine hundred troops training now, and the blacksmiths have been endlessly making more armor and weapons. If you ask me, he is up to no good."

The two looked at each other with concern. "Why, then, have there been so many offers of trade to the surrounding cities recently?"

She leaned forward and whispered, "Some say to find out what the neighboring regions need, and cut off their supply."

This immediately sparked a revelation in the scouts' minds; when Zekern had talked of peace and the expansion of fellow cities, he had been deceiving them. This news could change everything. Lord Auden must hear about this as soon as possible. The attack could be coming sooner than anticipated. If Zekern already had almost a thousand troops under his wing, he could be ready to strike soon.

They thanked the woman and left, looking for the rest of their team. Scanning the busy streets, their nerves skyrocketing, the two hurried about. The regular hustle and bustle of people obstructed their search. They needed to find their teammates. Something was wrong, terribly wrong.

The buildings around them seemed to hide all sorts of evil. Saberlin appeared less and less hospitable the longer their search lasted. Where were the rest of the scouts?

Suddenly, their fears were confirmed. Guards with spears extended surrounded a small group of men. Painfully, the two spies realized their comrades were captured. Their mission was finished. They must leave. They must leave now.

As the two headed out of Saberlin, the guards asked, "Where is the rest of your group?"

"They sent us back to care for our farms. We are not needed here any longer," they replied.

The guards were not convinced. "You seem a bit too young for this line of work. Where do you live?"

As the guards went to grab a hold of them, the spies sped off like rabbits into the forest. They stopped neither for water nor rest. They knew they were the only ones who could make it back to Hightenmore. The information they had gained would have to do. Their feet ached as if stung by many wasps, but they would not stop. Their running eventually slowed to jogging, their breaths sharp and short.

A squad of four knights dressed in black armor rode out of Saberlin on horseback to catch the criminals. At least, that is what they considered them to be. Their horses snorted furiously, upset that they had to race through the forest, dodging trees at a fast pace.

The two heard the hoof beats in the distance and ran through the mossy forest floor with undimmed determination. Their lungs throbbed, their feet bled, and their muscles ached, all while trying to see through tired eyes. The only things that guided them were fear and the steadfast compass of loyalty.

The men tried everything they could to lose their pursuers. They zigzagged in odd directions. They splashed into streams, then quickly rose out of them. Hopefully their enemies' horses would stop or at least slow at the water. They hurdled over bushes and dove through tight gaps between trees, anything to gain ground.

Soon they cleared the trees and were thrashed by the glare of blazing sunlight as they tumbled into the valley. As they ran, one of them collapsed on the ground. He picked himself up, knowing he must go on. Four horses galloped down after them. Four ominous swords were drawn. The knights eyed the two stragglers with fury as they neared the village outside of Hightenmore. As a fire consumes all in its path, Zekern's knights charged forward until the guards stationed there rushed upon them with swords and spears. The wicked knights tried to break through them, but soon retreated to the forest. They had blood on their swords, but not the blood they desired.

The two scouts were brought into Hightenmore, then carried into the castle since they were too exhausted to walk. Lord Auden and all who were with him rushed upon the two weary souls who had collapsed at the table. Kyra treated them immediately, while others gave them some food. Auden paused to give the scouts time to recover and to eat.

The scouts insisted on giving their report as soon as they could. They sat up and looked to the others as they told their story. "Lord Auden, we have recovered the information, but the others are trapped in the city and are presumed dead."

"Are you sure they didn't escape?" Auden asked.

"We watched them get captured, sir. They may still be alive, but I would doubt it."

Auden's expression grew grave. "Continue."

150

"We entered Saberlin and spent the night in the inn. In the morning, we split into groups as planned to find the information. After some prodding, an elderly woman told us that ever since becoming king, Zekern has been raising an army. He lied about wanting unity and developing new trade routes. He has brought his troops together in Saberlin for training and new armor. He has around nine hundred troops, and more may be training at the moment."

There were gasps throughout the room. Then they continued. "When we left, the guards said Zekern had ordered all horses to be brought to Saberlin, almost like a horse tax. So he will have a cavalry. We were chased down by riders, but the guards in the village fended them off. That is everything we know. We are not sure how large of an army Zekern will want before attacking. Perhaps it may be a month if he wants everyone armed and trained."

"So it is more serious than we expected," Lord Auden replied. "Send word to the nearest cities to see if they will supply troops. Meanwhile, have the villages prepare for an attack by the week's end. I want them ready once the alarm is sounded."

His advisors stood to leave the room. "It will be done, my lord," they said as they turned and rushed out.

CHAPTER 14

SIEGE

One week passed. Natas arrived at Saberlin under a veil of secrecy. He looked across the city with a critical glance, not passing over any detail. He wanted to make sure Saberlin was completely ready...ready to wage war against Hightenmore.

Natas knew that even if they succeeded in taking the mighty fortress to the north, Saberlin was still at risk of attack. It needed all defenses possible, even if only as a precaution.

The oblivious people hustling across the city streets made Natas grin deviously. No one even knew what was truly going on. No one fathomed the length of his wicked plot.

Natas was mildly impressed by the majestic stature of the castle. Nevertheless, he had seen higher walls and bigger cities. His own palace towered in comparison to this northwestern bastion, but in his greed he would never be satisfied. Riches could always be greater, beauty could always become more beautiful, power always needed to be exercised.

Ascending the stairs, he entered the doorway to Zekern's throne room. "Who are you, and what is your business with Lord Zekern?" the guards said almost robotically.

Instead of answering, Natas slipped off his black hood, revealing his crimson hair and dark, penetrating eyes. Under his cloak he wore a red robe, hoping it would give him a more powerful appearance. He looked as young as a teenager, but that was only a deception to hide his true form. Everything about his appearance screamed overlord and master. Rage and deceit emanated from his being.

The guards stepped back, almost cowering before him. Though they had never seen him before, they knew. "King Natas, we...we had no idea it was you. We did not hear of your arrival. Please forgive us." They immediately opened the doors and escorted him to Zekern's study. They quietly knocked on the door. No answer. They knocked harder. No answer. They banged loudly, embarrassed that they were not able to present their lord more quickly.

Finally, an answer came from within the study. It was determined and fierce. "You dolts! Did I not specifically tell you that I was not to be disturbed unless completely necessary?"

"But, lord..." the guards insisted.

Zekern harshly interrupted. "I do not want any of your foolish talk. I don't care who's there or what he wants. Just get them out of the throne room immediately."

Natas then addressed him. "Zekern, would you care if your King Natas was at the door?" It seemed to roll off his tongue like poison.

The door flung open. Zekern quickly knelt before Natas, his head on the floor in reverence. He dismissed his guards. "My master, I am sorry for delaying you. I...I did not know of your arrival. Come in, please. Where would you like to sit?"

"In the study is fine." After they had been seated, Natas continued. "I came here to remind you of our deal. A deal I hope you have not forgotten or dismissed. Do you remember that since I had my assassins skillfully finish your brother, a possible threat to your throne, you promised to raise an army and capture Hightenmore? The time to strike is upon us. It will be a win for both of us. It will sever the King of Light's empire, curse his name, and give you the trade routes and fertile coastlands you have always hungered after."

"I agree with everything you have said, but I don't understand. Why are you here? I am continuing as planned. My army is amassing numbers Hightenmore could never hope to withstand. I am ready to stab a dagger straight into their hearts. It will be a blow they can never recover from. Peace has lasted long enough. War is what I desire."

Natas was not swayed by Zekern's display. "I wish to see your army for inspection. I have brought engineers to construct the siege weapons necessary to break through the walls. Also, I have brought more metal for armor. Your soldiers had better be as skilled and brutal as you have claimed."

"As you wish, my king."

Zekern's general lined up the men for inspection around midday. The sun shone bright in the sky, blasting their armor with dreary heat. The men overcame their discomfort purely due to their fear of Natas. The common peasants were ushered outside the area, so no one except the soldiers could know what was happening.

Zekern and his master peered into the very souls of the warriors and critiqued them of any flaw, major or minor. They chose nine hundred troops out of the thousand as infantry, and one hundred skilled horsemen as cavalry. A few soldiers were re-armored and a few received newer, stronger weapons, discarding the old ones like rotten food.

Zekern knew that if he could get those horsemen inside the outer wall, they would have the upper hand. The horsemen would also make swift work of the guards and peasants in the villages. These heavily armored horsemen were Zekern's top fighting force.

He held his infantry in high regard, as well. Zekern forced them to swear their allegiance and demanded them to give nothing less than their best. He was sure the unsuspecting Hightenmore would fall beneath his grasp.

Zekern felt his power had always been underestimated. He wished that everyone who gazed upon him would bow to him. He longed to have his name written down in history as a mighty conqueror and a successful ruler.

His empire would grow, he could feel it. As anyone who knew him could instantly claim, he was prideful and strong-willed. He would not take no for an answer, especially since failing Natas meant instant trouble...the kind of trouble that permeates more than just the circumstance.

******

Meanwhile, in Hightenmore, Lord Auden was puzzled by the current events. There had been no price which Zekern wished them to pay to hold off the invasion. Auden sent a message of diplomatic terms to Zekern, but no reply came.

It seemed as if nothing would persuade Zekern otherwise. Auden knew some master plan was in play; was it just to confuse him, or possibly to distract him from other matters? He would not let it come to that. The preparations continued. Half of the villagers' produce was stored away in case anything was to go wrong.

Calix and the others trained steadily to become commanders of Auden's army. The trainers had set out a routine for the five: two hours of physical training, four hours of weapons training and one hour of strategic training. One part of their physical training included a challenge of strength. Two soldiers in armor tried to push each other to opposite ends of the room. Grax was unmatched in this exercise. The weapons training was a course of blocking, dodging and thrusting. Nadrian and the other archers practiced quickly drawing and firing their bows both short and long ranges. Felloni masterfully executed his course, rolling under the swinging dummies with ease. In the strategic training, each person was given a test designed to see how well they reacted to combat situations. Chan showed that he knew when it was best to attack and when best to retreat and resupply. Although the training was challenging, the five could see each other's skills improve.

On the opposite side of Hightenmore, Kyra also began her training. When she entered the doctor's house, the first thing she saw was a large shelf filled with vials. Kyra shuddered as she noticed leeches in one. A man stepped out from the back room. "Are you the new apprentice?" he asked.

"Yes, I am." She took off her bracelet and rolled up her sleeves. She learned quickly as her teacher instructed her in the various arts of medicine known at the time.

As much as Kyra tried to remain focused on her studies, she could not help but worry about Hightenmore's progress. Lord Auden was doing all that he could; she only hoped that it would be enough. She knew first-hand the threat that Zekern posed.

Time marched on. Archers were posted. Weapons were crafted and sharpened. On the fifth of April, an emissary was received from the Lord of Vanswick, a nearby city. His message read, "The Lord of Vanswick, your dear friend, has remembered your willingness to send medicine to his people in their time of trial. Now he intends to return the favor by sharing the new-found technology of crossbows. He is giving you these advanced crossbows and an engineer to help you make even more. Several large carts of food and a unit of crossbowmen accompany the engineer. The Lord of Vanswick would have provided foot troops and additional supplies, but he could not mobilize them in time to make the journey. It would have taken a couple of weeks for such a feat. Sending all his troops would have also made Vanswick unprotected if Zekern turned his focus on it instead. However, the Lord of Vanswick hopes the King's blessings will protect you."

The engineer was shown to the blacksmith's shop, where he skillfully demonstrated the art of making the high-powered, armor piercing crossbows. He spent all day there, and the fire was stoked upon the ashes continually.

The next day, Auden's best archers were taught to use the crossbows. Although they were heavier, they provided sharper aim, longer distance and enough power to shoot an arrow clean through a board at fifty steps. The emissary was quick to leave, for his job was simply to bring the message. The engineer, though, stayed many days, discussing with Lord Auden the progress on the crossbows and news of the recent affairs of Vanswick. The archers from Vanswick also remained to train Auden's men and to protect Hightenmore when the time came.

Auden was glad to hear from his commanders that they now had six hundred armed troops. Yet he knew Zekern's army would be rallying also, and many of Auden's troops were not full-time soldiers. So the training, arming and locating of troops would need to continue, and all the faster.

Auden knew the castle would have a strong chance to survive, yet he was afraid for the villages outside the walls. While he did not want to put his troops at risk outside the safety of Hightenmore, he also did not want to leave the villages unguarded. He made a thoughtful yet urgent decision. All women and children would need to come inside the walls until the siege was over. They would have to cram into houses or wherever room could be found, but at least they would be safer than outside the walls.

******

The new day was bright, the air fresh, and the castle was gleaming in the sun's full light. Hightenmore seemed to glisten in the array as pure silver. Auden stood from his balcony, admiring the fair castle. He could not let this fortress of light fall to Zekern's dark hand.

Suddenly a horn sounded, long and low, throughout the castle from a nearby village. Then the bell towers from the villages rang, confirming their fear: Zekern's troops were coming.

The entire castle flung into action; they knew Zekern's forces would be there in a matter of minutes. The newly forged weapons were dispersed amongst the troops. Swords and shields, axes and spears, arrows and maces were retrieved as soldiers rushed to their posts. Archers grabbed their crossbows and knelt on the outer wall, waiting for Nadrian's command. She had the honor of being assigned as their leader. She had decided to stick with her longbow, since it was more natural for her.

Zekern's forces were led by his general. The commander's armor was riddled with spikes, giving him a menacing appearance. His forces had six battering rams which were each manned by eight soldiers. If one of those battering rams reached a gate, wave upon wave of enemies would roll into Hightenmore. Hightenmore would be crushed like a castle made of sand, not stone. In addition to the battering rams, Zekern's forces used an advanced shield formation which minimized damage, although it cut the soldiers' speed.

They slowly marched closer and closer to the castle. Zekern's soldiers were brutal, slaughtering men left and right as they trampled through the villages. Some farmers tried to fight back, but their pitchforks and other make-shift weapons did little damage. Sadly, dozens of villagers were killed before they reached safety.

The troops were not interested in plundering the villages; rather, they continued toward the castle in formation. "Fire!" Nadrian yelled as she and her archers flung arrows at the enemy. The large mounted crossbows inflicted the most damage, and helped destroy some of the battering rams.

Only one battering ram survived, but it managed to reach the southern gate. With its first swing, the gate shook and splintered, but held fast. The archers above it shot down the soldiers preparing for a second swing, but more men took their place. These adversaries lifted the battering ram and sent it charging into the gate. It barely survived the assault. Another volley of arrows was about to be sent upon it, but enemy archers shot down many of the archers above the gate. With a mighty effort, the third swing of the battering ram sent bits of wood flying from its wrath. An echoing crash sounded through the castle as the gate plummeted to the ground.

Zekern's remaining troops rushed passed the outer wall, catching Auden's soldiers off guard. The fighting was unorganized, as ranks of dark soldiers rushed past the outer wall. Most of the forces of light retreated to safety behind the inner wall. Those protecting the outer wall, however, fought with valor to their last breath, until they were overrun. They bought with their sacrifice precious time for the defenders on the inner wall.

The good news was that Zekern's men had not broken past this yet. The catapults helped greatly as they launched boulders onto the attackers. The enemy archers lit arrows on fire and shot them at the catapults. The soldiers ran for water, but they were too late. The catapults, which had destroyed the last battering ram and fired terror upon the enemy, were now encompassed in a blazing flame.

Still, the forces of light fought to prevent the oncoming assailants. Spears were hurled upon Zekern's men as they tried to break down the gate. Archer towers filled with crossbowmen tried to stop the assault. It was an unyielding attack, as Zekern's general sought to rampage through the inner gate as if it was not even there. His men were armed with great hammers specifically designed by Natas' engineers to shatter the gate. Those soldiers of darkness who were not shot down pounded on the gate with a drive that was almost senseless. Although the forces of evil lost dozens of men, the inner gate was finally broken through.

The enemy had so quickly gained an advantage that it was apparent many would now die as they flooded in. Auden's heart sank as he saw his men falling in battle. Zekern's cavalry charged the men of light, their iron hoof prints spreading terror upon their foes. At first, the front line of Hightenmore was overwhelmed by the numerous enemies assailing them, but Calix rallied them. He called them together, and they assumed formation, just as they had been trained.

Calix was at the front of the force guarding the gateway and raised his weapon to meet the foe; he slashed and blocked, stopping the oncoming enemies. Many foes tried to break past him, but his years of training in the forest had not left him defenseless. He remembered Lavrin, and fought all the harder to honor his captive friend.

Calix was at the front of the arrowhead formation they had formed. The troops rallied under his example as he bravely faced his foes. He could not see the impact he was making in the larger scale of the battle. The soldiers of the light were unyielding to the forces of darkness. Calix continued to fight, though he did not realize that he was becoming more and more surrounded.

He lasted in the heat of the battle as long as he could, but the onslaught plowed into him, and he could not keep his footing. He fell to the ground, only to see an enemy warrior standing above him. Try as he might, Calix could not block the axe which plunged into his chest, piercing his heart. "May... the King... reign," he cried out, "and his... followers..." But as his blood flowed and death swept over him, he could not finish the final word.

"Calix! No!" At the sight of his fallen friend, Grax was filled with fury. He bashed the oncoming foes with all his might. He would not let Calix die in vain.

Despite Calix's heroic stand, Auden's men retreated to the castle. Grax would have continued fighting near the inner wall if Chan had not pulled him back. Grax followed Chan to the castle, expecting the battle to follow them in. Instead of barging in, the invaders waited...waited for Auden's men to come out of their safe haven. All remaining weapons were dispersed among the men of the light. Although few were left to carry them, they clung to their hope in the King. The battle for their home was far from over.

The soldiers of Hightenmore went out to meet the enemy. There would be one final stand. If the invaders would not come to them, they would go to the invaders. Lord Auden held his long sword in front of him; on his shield was the emblem of the King. He rallied his faithful men. "Although they surround us, let us not be known to have given up this fight. Remember all that the King means to you, and remember all he has done for you. Warriors, may this castle once again be a refuge of hope and glory!"

Grax charged ahead with his weapons swinging mightily. He met the soldiers who challenged him with zeal and, using all his might, tossed them to the ground. Felloni used his training to dodge numerous attacks. He finished several foes by throwing his daggers before they could raise their shields. Felloni jumped onto one foe, stabbed him in the neck and leaped to the ground, blocking a sword thrust with the spikes on his gloves. Chan and Auden were directing the soldiers into a formation around the castle with spears extended and shields up. Archers rose behind the crouching soldiers, steadily releasing a barrage of arrows. Nadrian was leading them, firing her arrows at anyone who dared to near her. Though the shields were rammed from all sides, the soldiers stood firm. Like an ocean tide, back and forth the battle raged.

Arrows came upon them from all sides. Grax and Felloni were back to back, slaying anyone who neared them. Nadrian kept her arrows flying, but soon found that she only had a few left, including the one from Lord Auden. The arrow volley from both sides wounded many soldiers. Felloni took an arrow to the arm but managed to keep fighting.

Zekern's forces took many casualties, but Auden knew his soldiers could not hold such open ground. Nadrian blew her horn loudly before she was forced back into the castle. Felloni rushed toward the castle with all haste, with Grax right behind him.

The narrow hallways were highly defendable because only a few soldiers could enter at once. The soldiers of the light did not let the invaders keep them pinned in the castle. Zekern's troops were used to open-field battle, but within the halls of the castle, they were no match to Auden's men. They instantly regretted charging in. The men of light were gaining ground. They continued to push back their foes farther and farther from the halls. The tide of battle seemed to be shifting in their favor.

Chan once more made a formation out of the remaining soldiers. He fought as he directed, taking on charging enemies with ease. Chan blocked an axe, spun to the side, and left the adversary lying on the ground. Lord Auden gathered his soldiers and, with shields raised, bashed the oncoming foes. Tables, barrels and other items were brought from inside the castle to barricade the doorway. Archers from both sides launched arrows upon their enemies till their quivers were empty. Grax and Felloni gave all they had, both physically and mentally, to reach their friends. Through skill, speed, and a bit of luck, they dove behind the barricade and regrouped with their friends inside the citadel.

Sadly, the barricade could not hold the determined enemies of Hightenmore. As fast as it had been assembled, the barricade was destroyed. Chaos broke loose within the castle. Nadrian, Chan and Lord Auden fought together, but knew they could not hold out for long. There was nothing they could do but fall back. "Retreat to the hall!" Lord Auden closed the broad doors just as they was slammed against by a horde of warriors.

Auden looked into the eyes of the remaining defenders of Hightenmore. Their spirits had failed them, and their wounds were many. He longed to comfort them, but felt his own courage beginning to dwindle. They had lost both inner and outer walls, and had nowhere left to turn. Was this it? Was it all over?

As hope diminished and Zekern's men advanced into the hall, a bright flash stunned everyone, and an angel, glowing like the sun, descended from the sky. His eyes were like gems and his sword was brighter than a hundred torches. His blade was made of blue, white and red fire with a handle of glistening gold and precious jewels.

With a single swing of his sword, the angel destroyed most of Zekern's army. The wave of fire enveloped them, killing them in seconds. In a flash, he returned to the sky. The King's mighty warrior had come to them in their most desperate hour. The battle had turned.

Amazed by what he had just witnessed, Auden knew that the King had seen their plight. He had not only seen their need, but he had saved them from it. He had not only given them hope, but a chance to finish the battle. The army of the light was no longer broken, but was forged by the mighty fire of the angel's sword.

Auden knew he needed to capitalize on this advantage. He sent soldiers to sneak through the tunnels to surprise the enemy. Leading the group, Chan was ready to give his all to protect his friends and honor the sacrifice of Calix and those already fallen. Chan's group ascended from the tunnels and ambushed the enemy with a speed that was unheard of. Zekern's men were trapped.

As Zekern's general scrambled to get his troops back in fighting formation, Nadrian drew her last arrow. She walked a few steps to the left, making sure she had the perfect angle. Her silver arrow flew with speed and met the heart of Zekern's general.

As their leader fell, the remaining attackers were thrown into confusion. Only a few of them survived, and they fled in every direction, caring only for their own lives. They fled the castle and rushed past the villages in the Avrick Valley, dropping their weapons and casting off their armor. They did not even realize that no one was chasing them.

*****

Felloni picked up Calix's sword and carefully placed it upon him as his body was taken away. He could

167

not say anything. He should have been there to save him. Felloni did not dwell on the notion, though, knowing it was not what Calix would have wanted.

Kyra and a few other doctors knelt on the scorched grass, healing the wounded. It would take them many hours to treat all the injured men. The other survivors gathered together and lifted praises to the King for sending his mighty angel in their time of need.

Auden looked upon the same city he had admired that very morning. It still held some of its grandeur; its walls were intact and its people were praising the King. Overall, however, so much of its beauty had been lost. Buildings were now nothing more than rubble, and hundreds of citizens would never take another breath. "How did I let this happen?" Auden asked Chan, who was standing beside him. "I'm afraid that I have failed my people greatly this day. Without the aid of the King, we would have been utterly destroyed."

"Nothing could be further from the truth, my lord."

Auden turned toward him. "How can you believe that, when you've seen the destruction Zekern's men have done?"

"I do not see the men you have lost, but rather the men you have saved. Look at their faces. They are proud of our victory, and proclaiming the name of the King like they have never done before. Word of Zekern's defeat will spread across the land, inspiring thousands. We have made a great blow at Natas' efforts, the first of many, I hope. Do not be troubled by what could have been. We have no time to think of what could have been when the King is calling us to look ahead… to look ahead and see all the good that will come from this day. Now come, help me carry the wounded."

CHAPTER 15

SILENT RESCUE

During the siege, a secret mission was underway in Saberlin. Only a few guards were left at its towering walls because of the attack. The seven spies lowered their hoods and tightly gripped their ropes. At the end of these cords, sharp hooks of metal were attached like talons.

With utmost silence, the group sneaked up to Saberlin's high walls and leaned against them. They peered upward and noticed that five guards were pacing above. Luckily, the guards had their eyes fixated outward, not directly below.

Seven grappling hooks soared up above the wall in the dead of night and latched on. With a firm grasp, the skilled invaders climbed with steadfast determination until they reached the top. They unlatched the hooks and let the ropes fall back to the ground. Brandishing their short swords, the men knelt low and crept toward the oblivious guards. The five protectors of Saberlin fell without a cry piercing the air.

The seven took a deep breath. They were inside. Dragging the bodies behind an old building, three of the men put on the armor of the sentries. It was the perfect disguise, especially without sunlight to differentiate one face from another.

An air of success swept about the invaders, yet they pushed it aside. They had not finished yet. They had not saved the prisoners.

Reaching the prison towers in a matter of minutes, they quieted their minds. They needed absolute focus to convince these guards they were the watchmen. Fortunately, the prison keepers outside the towers were already distracted. Four of them could barely keep their eyes open. The other six were bent over a table muttering about some high-stakes game.

A bold man, cloaked in his disguise, went toward the group without emotion. "I have four prisoners here who I need to lock up." The other two disguised men dragged their four companions into the torchlight.

The guards were so enthralled in their game that it was a while before they answered. One of the men shot the spy an angry glance. "Go talk to the jail warden," he sneered. He shot his finger out toward a man to their right.

Sauntering to the warden, the man cringed at his bruised face and scarred arms. A long whip lay in his hands, and his eyes flashed open as the spy approached.

The warden gave the unassuming man a hostile expression which caught him off guard. Nevertheless, he stepped toward the warden. "Where should I place these enemies of Zekern?"

"What is their crime?"

The man paused. "We caught them stealing food from Lord Zekern's private storehouses."

The warden turned his eyes toward the four men. "I see. You fellows just cannot be content with the food Lord Zekern has set before you? I would spit on you, but my throat is awfully dry this evening."

"They are serious trouble makers. I believe they should be separated to different ends of the dungeon. Do you have cuffs so we can restrain them properly?"

The warden called to a man a few yards away who brought a coarse rope to bind them. "I can take them from here. You men should return to your posts. We can't have anyone sneaking into our city while we're unaware."

"That would be awful," they answered. "We should take them, though. They are quick-tempered." To prove their point, the tied captives began to wildly struggle against their holders. After several of the sentinels rushed to help restrain them, the prisoners stopped resisting.

172

The four vicious captives were separated and dragged into the dungeon. The warden handed keys to both groups of guards. "You'll need these."

After entering the filthy jail, the invaders easily overwhelmed the tired, unfocused guards. The guards were then bound and thrown into the cells meant for the food thieves. Quickly, the spies searched the dungeon. In the eastern corner, four of the men spied Lavrin sleeping on the stone floor.

"Wake up!" they whispered, and he rose to his feet.

After trying several keys, they unlocked his cell and released him of his shackles. They assured him that they followed the King and handed him a blade they had snatched from the guards.

After freeing the other followers of the King, the assembly left the dungeon. As if mice sneaking by a resting cat, the large group crept passed the sentinels with utmost precaution. They then wove through shadowy paths like a snake, until they reached a large, spreading oak. The escapees began to climb out of the city one by one. Prying eyes from Saberlin's watchmen were few and spread thin, so reaching the top of the wall was simple.

They then began descending the wall with the help of tangled vines. Near the end of the line, Lavrin noticed something familiar about the tree as he planted his boots on a solid branch. It was the same tree Felloni had used to climb out of Saberlin with the manuscripts. Lavrin ran his hand over the smooth bark and contemplated. "It surely would be a crime if such a marvelous tree was ever chopped down."

As Lavrin reached the height of the oak, a watchman's gaze turned straight toward him. Instinctively, Lavrin dropped to his chest in the leaves. Luckily, the darkness concealed him amongst the foliage and the sentinel continued his rounds. The group successfully left Saberlin and fled to the forest.

A dark green litz, the one which had brought Lavrin the message, flew to the head ranger and landed on his shoulder. As he stroked its scales, the ranger said to Lavrin, "I am Isilmus. My litz brought you my message. We are now to take you to Hightenmore. The King of Light has seen your faithfulness. You will need to move very quickly to reach Hightenmore in time. We will escort the other prisoners there as well, but you should travel on ahead of us. They are expecting you."

"Thank you, friend, for your courage and loyalty. I am truly in your debt. Hopefully, I will see you again in the near future." Lavrin ran ahead of the group, wondering exactly what he needed to be on time for.

******

Lavrin finally ascended the steps into the Great Hall of Hightenmore Castle. It had been a difficult journey, striding from shadow to shadow like a common criminal. Although his wounds lingered, he was hopeful that he would find peace here. Most of all, he looked forward to seeing Calix again.

174

Lord Auden looked up from the grand book Felloni had lent him. "Hello, Lavrin. I've been awaiting your arrival. Your friends are in a room above. You may go and see them."

Moments later, Lavrin walked into the large room through a carved wooden door. He witnessed the group gathered around a small table, eating.

Lavrin slowly walked over to them. He held back until he could restrain himself no longer. "Did you save any for me?"

They all turned around. "Lavrin! You're here!" Kyra exclaimed. "We thought we might never see you again."

"Lord Auden's rangers saved me from the jaws of Saberlin. While I was prisoner there, I constantly dreamed of being able to see you all again. I certainly never thought I would be able to walk down Hightenmore's halls with you. What's happened here? The Avrick Valley is as black as a raven."

Felloni had just finished describing the fateful attack when one of Lord Auden's guards knocked on the door. He wore a long green cape over his armor, held a crossbow at his side, and had a sword sheathed on his back. When the door was opened, he stepped in. "You are wanted in the hall," he said, then departed.

With arms around each other's shoulders, Chan and Lavrin headed toward the hall. They talked mostly of

175

Lavrin's time in Saberlin. He told Chan about the followers of the King he had met during his captivity. Chan stopped Lavrin a few steps before entering the hall. "Lavrin, there is something I must tell you."

Lavrin raised an eyebrow. "Yes?"

"Calix did not make it through the battle. He fought hard and died proclaiming the name of the King."

Lavrin turned and looked down the hallway behind them. "You can come out now, Calix. I'm not going to fall for that so easily."

Chan bit his lip as Lavrin looked back toward him. A tear rolled down Lavrin's cheek. Chan glanced at the ground, unable to look Lavrin in the face. "I am so sorry, Lavrin. I know how much he meant to you. He died an honorable death, and his bravery will not be forgotten."

"At least he did not die in vain." Lavrin forced out the words. "I hope I can live in a way that honors his legacy." They descended the stone stairway, and were the last to arrive in the hall. Lavrin barely fought back a snowstorm of emotions.

Auden waited for Lavrin and Chan to stand beside their companions. "My friends, this journey is ending, but a new one may yet begin." They all exchanged glances. He continued. "The gracious King of Light has seen the hardships you have faced and the loyalty you have shown. You have gone to great lengths to promote the light in Amcronos. He has decided to offer you a rare gift – a chance to enter the Haven Realm. A ship has just arrived in the harbor to take you there."

Grax stepped forward. "Lord, we are unworthy to do so."

"No one is truly worthy of such a gift, but the King gives it anyway. You have followed him faithfully and sacrificed much. Thankfully, perfection is not necessary."

"Thank you, Lord Auden. I have always wished to be reunited with those I have lost. I cannot wait to see their faces again. I will enter the Haven Realm if the King would have me."

"I know that I do not deserve this blessing," Nadrian said. "Yet, I am not sure if I could depart from all that I hold dear here."

"I have heard that the Haven Realm is similar to Amcronos in many ways, yet all is pure and right there," Auden answered. "It has none of the evils of this land. I will not force you to decide either way; the choice is yours."

"I will praise the King forever for letting me enter his land," Nadrian continued.

Felloni had a different reply. "I wish not to upset you, but I believe I'm still needed in Amcronos. There are enemies to vanquish and people who need hope."

Auden looked into his eyes and saw a drive and purpose that outweighed all else. "You mean well. This is a hard choice for you, Felloni, but I tell you: always remember the King, and he will help you. I will be here to help as much as I can. I know that you will always be an encouragement to the King's followers."

Felloni looked at his friends, and then hugged each of them. They offered him the gifts they had received from Lord Auden. "We won't need these anymore."

"Please remind Macrollo of me, and give him my thanks," Felloni replied. "Tell Calix that though I only knew him a short while, I considered him a close friend. I know the road ahead will be tough, but there are many things I still wish to do in the King's name. Besides, who else would keep these precious gifts?"

Lavrin then bowed before Auden. "My lord, many people have wished for such a generous opportunity, but I also believe my work is not done here. My time in Saberlin allowed me to see that the King has a greater purpose in store for me. I would never wish for Felloni to take this burden on alone. Although I deeply wish to reunite with Calix, I want to honor his memory by remaining here. Anyways, you will need help rebuilding Hightenmore."

Chan had not expected this. "Are you sure, friends? The Haven Realm awaits us. We could see wonders beyond imagination."

Felloni responded with his typical, slow nod. Lavrin, however, answered him. "I am very glad you have the chance to journey to the Haven Realm. It is a land beyond description. However, the brutal slavery in Saberlin still haunts me. There are evils in this world that must be brought down at all costs. I will see you again someday."

"If it be your desire," Lord Auden said in reply. "I will have you knighted under Hightenmore's banner as your friends have been."

"That would be an honor. I can only hope that the darkness of this land will someday tremble before the banner of the light."

Kyra waited till there was silence before answering. "Lavrin has shown me the importance of following the King. I wish for my parents also to receive this joy. I have finally found the purpose for my life and now need to live it out. What good is finding your purpose if you do not fulfill it? Felloni, Lavrin, count me in on your quest. We will redeem Amcronos."

"Yes, help will be needed, if we are to spread the truth and stand against Natas," Felloni said. "It will be difficult, and we will need to do whatever it takes to follow the King."

Lavrin, Felloni and Kyra gathered close to their comrades and hugged them tightly. Felloni and Grax looked deeply into each other's eyes, remembering all the heartache and loss they had endured together. Truly, they were of one mind and spirit. They had fought with their lives to save Hightenmore, and had succeeded.

"Farewell, man of mighty strength," Felloni said to Grax.

"Farewell, man of silent bravery," Grax replied, fighting back a wellspring of emotions.

Lavrin and Chan shook hands firmly. "You are an amazing leader," Lavrin told him. "You ought to be proud of the example you have set."

"Except for the time I imprisoned one of the most worthy men I've ever encountered."

Lavrin grinned. "I forgave you for that long ago."

Chan took off an ornate, silver token from under his cloak and handed it to Lavrin. "You lead the Silent Watchers now. Take care of Kyra - she is truly precious. Remember Felloni means the best at heart. He always does."

Lavrin leaned in close to Chan. "Please tell Calix these words when you see him: the sparrow and the blue jay have made a home together. Express kindness to him however you can, for it is his friendship that has given me strength all these years."

Nadrian and Kyra sat together beside a tall pillar at the far end of the hall. They gazed toward their four comrades exchanging farewells. "I suppose this is goodbye. Promise me you will never stop healing others."

"Of course," Kyra replied. "Promise me that you will save me a seat at your table when I arrive in the Haven Realm someday."

"Of course," Nadrian said likewise.

"Make sure Macrollo knows we succeeded and that his letter saved Hightenmore. I will never forget getting to know a talking leopard."

"I will never forget the first time he spoke to us. I will make sure he knows that his efforts saved our lives. Hopefully, I can last the voyage there. The last time I set foot on a boat, I became sick after five minutes."

"With a heart like yours, nothing can stop you from fulfilling your desires," Kyra said.

They both rose and embraced each other. Nadrian knew she would miss Kyra for a long while. "I could say the same to you," Nadrian told her.

******

Nadrian, Grax, Chan, Kyra, Felloni and Lavrin followed Lord Auden to the harbor. All was quiet as the lighthouse began its evening watch. A silver ship was docked in the harbor. The three masts and their sails were pure gold. The sails spread out like dragon's wings. The main sail had the emblem of the King in brilliant display. On the massive boat's side was written:

The Light Speed

The wind blew toward the Haven Realm to the west. They would have perfect sailing.

The six were dressed in purple robes, and those who had gathered at the harbor proclaimed them as heroes and honored their achievements. They then lifted as one voice the motto of the King. "The great King of Light, may he live and reign forever, and may his followers prosper."

They passed through a row of soldiers who bowed to them, and as they neared The Light Speed, horns were blasted in their honor. The song of the horns had an air of majestic purity. Birds tweeted softly in the willow trees beside the harbor.

Inside the castle, the swords of Chan, Nadrian and Grax were placed in a glass display in the central hall. They were put in a prominent place so that many could find hope in their story. An engraved plaque was made to pay tribute to their lives and their bravery. That way, anyone who entered Hightenmore's grand hall could remember the historic day that Saberlin's army was defeated.

Nadrian knew she would miss her friends and Vin's small, cheerful eyes. She knew that everyone must leave Amcronos when they die, but now she would not have to die as Macrollo and Calix had. She, Chan and Grax had been given a rare opportunity indeed. Nadrian took the first step onto The Light Speed, followed by Chan and Grax. She turned back as it left the harbor. She waved to Lavrin, Felloni and Kyra, and they waved back. Lavrin saw relief and peace in the three pairs of distant eyes.

They were three warriors on a massive ship, ornate far beyond the skill of any craftsman, heading through waters as still as the air. No sailors guided the boat onward; it moved westward as if it had a mind of its own. The Light

Speed was lost in a shroud of mist that covered the ocean as far as the eye could see. The citizens took rose petals and lay them on the waters as a sign of their gratitude. Hundreds of blossoms rode the waves ever westward.

As Chan, Grax and Nadrian entered the Haven Realm, they were made perfect, and came to see wonders unknown even in man's wildest dreams. Everything was wonderful and whole. Enjoying a land filled with many marvels, they were free from evil and experienced fellowship with all the others who had loved the King, as well. They were reunited with Macrollo and Calix, who led them to a banquet at the King's table. Calix cried many tears of joy when Chan retold him Lavrin's message. Many days and nights were spent together remembering the old days in Amcronos and the King's faithfulness in their lives.

******

Felloni, Lavrin and Kyra returned to their rooms with heavy hearts. They knew they had done the hard, yet right thing and were at peace with their decision. They also were glad they had one another to lean on in times of trouble, and of course, Vin to cheer them up. The three knew the King would be with them and looked forward to the adventures he had in store for them.

AFTERWORD

Lavrin entered the burial grounds and found his way to Calix's resting place. He knelt beside it, struggling to find the words to say. "Calix, I know you have found your way to a better place. I wish I could see you one more time. We have so much to talk about. I hear you died a warrior's death. I would expect nothing less from such a faithful friend. Make sure you know your way around the place by the time I get there, because I'll expect a full tour."

Felloni and Kyra watched him from a distance. "Do you think he'll be alright?" Kyra longed to ease his pain.

"Give him some time. This wound will not be an easy one to heal."

They waited until their forlorn companion retired to a nearby bench. They came to him as he sat admiring his new sword. It was masterfully crafted, and had a dragon on the hilt. It was Lavrin's gift for being knighted into

Hightenmore's army. The three scrolled through the purple and golden book which told of the King's followers. When they turned the page of the last story, they found many new pages which were blank.

They recalled both the joys and the hardships of their lives and together added their stories. It took them several days, but they were glad to spend the time together. Lavrin wrote the stories of his, Kyra's and Calix's lives, while Felloni recalled the rest. Kyra drew pictures of their adventures, and Felloni drew maps of Amcronos and Hightenmore. Then the three rose, ready to start a new journey.

******

Zekern, Natas and the Lord of Srayo sat together at a table near a fire. Natas scornfully peered at Zekern. "I gave you everything you needed for success. How did you fail?"

"They…they had an angel who was sent from the King. We had the upper hand and broke through both walls but…"

"Be quiet! I have heard enough. Although this battle is lost, we still have Saberlin. My empire is strong. I must call on my ancient creatures to defeat such a being of the King. That angel will not bother us again."

The Lord of Srayo laughed heartily. It was a laugh void of sympathy and kindness. "Let's see what that cursed King does about that."

Noticing the change of tone, Zekern tried to share a bit of good news. "My King Natas, I do have splendid news, though. The town of Ken Van has a new gang in charge, and they want to join us. Best of all, the King of Light knows nothing of this."

Natas turned to him. "If this is so, we must exploit this gain before he finds out. Send a messenger to Ken Van immediately."

AUTHORS NOTE

Following the King is like following God. Jesus Christ lived a sinless life on this earth and died on a cross to free you from your bondage in sin. If you simply admit you have done wrong, believe that Jesus died for you and follow him through your life, you will enter heaven someday as Calix, Nadrian, Chan, Grax and Macrollo went to the Haven Realm.

You may say, "Well, I've never sinned." Have you ever lied or stolen? Have you ever dishonored your parents? These are all sin. Yet, like the King, God always finds ways to love us and forgive us of our wrongs.

If you want Christ in your life, you can say something like this: "Lord, I'm sorry I have done wrong. I know you love me and died for me on a cross. I am willing to follow you all of my days." This will not make your life perfect, but it will give you hope of a perfect future after death. God says in the Bible that he will never leave you or forsake you, and also to put on the armor of God to fight against evil. If you have a Bible, I encourage you to read it. It has changed my life. Try to gather together with other believers as knights gather to aid each other in battle.

If you are already a Christian, I pray that you never give up on your dreams and do everything you do for the glory of Jesus Christ. It may be tough, but God has given us what we need to continue in this journey of life, and if you strive in the Lord's power, you can win the battles. The great King of Light, may he live and reign forever, and may his followers prosper! God bless.

Made in the USA
Lexington, KY
11 April 2017